The Map of Us

S. A. Fanning

IMMORTAL WORKS
SALT LAKE CITY

Immortal Works LLC
1505 Glenrose Drive
Salt Lake City, Utah 84104
Tel: (385) 202-0116

© 2023 Pete Fanning
www.petefanning.com

Cover Art by Ashley Literski
http://strangedevotion.wixsite.com/strangedesigns

All rights reserved, including the right to reproduce this book or portions thereof in any form whatsoever. For more information visit https://www.immortalworks.press/contact.

This book is a work of fiction. Names, characters, businesses, organizations, places, events and incidents either are the product of the author's imagination or are used fictitiously. Any resemblance to actual persons, living or dead, events, or locales is entirely coincidental.

ISBN 978-1-953491-47-3 (Paperback)
ASIN B0BPQK8RXK (Kindle)

For Anne

Chapter 1

Mr. Hammock's truck creaks and groans with each sack of fertilizer I load onto the bed. Between trips from the truck to the pallet I wipe the sweat from my forehead, pat the dust from my jeans, while trying not to think too much about the side effects of breathing in all the toxic fumes. All the while, Mr. Hammock lauds the history of farm and tractor supply stores. No Lowes for that guy. No sir, you can't corporate-chain good old-fashioned customer service.

Around the fifteenth or sixteenth sack I've all but tuned him out, cursing him in my head for coming in so late with such a big order. My mind wanders, and I have to stop and recount. The old man never misses a beat. "...these big box stores come around and close things down. All about a profit margin for them..."

Sack twenty-four lands in place like a puzzle piece. I shut the tailgate, clear my throat. "Well, that should do it."

He turns, removes his hat, and dabs his forehead with a dingy handkerchief. His lips move as he counts, eyes jumping from one sack to the next. "Is that all of them?"

"Yes, sir."

Another cough, nod, and recount. What could this guy want with twenty-four fifty-pound bags of fertilizer? I guess it doesn't matter, he's satisfied, reaching for his wallet. "You boys got a big year ahead of you."

I hide my sigh with a cough. "Yes, sir."

"A few breaks and you might get back the playoffs."

"Yep."

He lingers for a minute, eager to talk Maycomb High football—

how it's been on a slide for years but now seems to be back on the cusp. I'd almost rather hear him crank up about profit margins again. Finally, he plucks a five from the battered billfold and hands it to me. "Well, good luck this week. Don't work too hard."

He gets a kick out of that, how hard I'm working, laughing and carrying on as he climbs into his truck and sets off on his way. I stuff the five in my pocket, clap the residue from my hands, and pick up the broom.

There's straw everywhere. Where did I put the dustpan, anyway? I start sweeping up a pile. My stomach grumbles, and I'm hoping Mom doesn't have a back-to-school meeting tonight so I can get a real dinner instead of something from the freezer. Dustpan. There it is, behind a bale of straw. I bend down to pick it up.

"Oh, yard boy."

The sound of her voice pitches me forward. I nearly go head over heels before I catch my balance and whirl around. My gaze climbs with wonder, from the sneakers to the smooth shapely legs, to the tight fitting t-shirt, and eventually to a face I've dreamed about almost every night for the past three years.

Another stumble, this time back a step as I wipe my eyes, fix my hair, and stand before her. Lia's smile drops, and her eyes widen. I can't say what my face is doing because I'm not sure that what I'm seeing is real.

She recovers with a laugh. "Hi," she says with a little wave, like she's been gone for a weekend.

It's been three years.

"Where?" I sputter, and barely manage that much. There's so much to ask, and I only have one mouth. *Where* is a good place to start, though. Where is this place with no phones, internet, or even a post office? But I only get out the *where* before Lia's smile leaves her face, and her mouth makes an O. She stares without blinking, her amazing eyes glittering as they search mine. We stand like that, a few feet apart, gawking at each other. There is a sea of gawk between us.

I open my mouth to try again, but she beats me to it.

"Sorry, I'm looking for Matthew Crosby?" Her eyes narrow, chin falling as she makes a show of looking me over again before shrugging with mock confusion, as though I need reminding of how there is no one else like her. She twirls a tress of hair, kicks out a sneaker. "Is he around?"

Three years ago the most amazing summer of my life ended abruptly one night, when Lia took off without a goodbye. And now, here she is. Taller, older, *curvier*, but every bit as magical.

I snap out of my trance, hook a thumb to the door. "I'll have to check," I say, trying to play along like she taught me so long ago. "Matthew, you said?"

She breaks first, squinting at me. "You're on the *football* team? Really?"

I restrain myself from jumping up and down, from launching into her with a hug. Instead, I shake my head, and the questions—white water rapids—flood my mind all over again. I reach for one. "What are you doing here?"

Again, it's not exactly what I want to say or how I want to say it, but I'm lucky to be saying anything at all considering I'm still swaying, eyeing a pallet of mulch for a place to land.

She closes her eyes and smiles. As I regain my footing, covered in dust and straw, I realize how badly my memory has failed me. Sure, I remember Lia being pretty, her eyes some unique kaleidoscope of hazel-gold sparkle. But now, here, with this living, breathing version—how the hue of her light brown skin contrasts with her white t-shirt—I realize nothing I memorized did a bit of justice to her smile, which is no less powerful than a lighthouse beacon.

She looks over her shoulder. "Well, I was going to buy some fertilizer, but it looks like that guy in the truck just bought it all." Again she looks me up and down. "Is that how you got so...big? Loading bags in trucks?"

I take a step closer to her without worrying how sweaty I am or what I must look like. How I smell.

She closes the distance with a tight hug, tighter than I was expecting. "How have you been?"

Vanilla. A hint of some herbal shampoo. She holds onto me, and a million moments dance their way through my nostrils and tickle my brain. Lia said she would return, and now here she is, after I'd convinced myself it would never happen. After I'd finally moved on. Or have I? Feeling her in my arms, nothing seems as important as her body—strong yet thin, perfect—against me.

In that hug, in that gust of memory-inducing vanilla, I momentarily forget where I am, *who* I am, and we're still locked in our embrace when the back door squeaks open and Mr. Yearly steps out to the loading dock.

"Hey, Matt, we've—"

I shoot away from Lia. She steps back and flashes Mr. Yearly a smile. He stammers over whatever he was going to say, but the look on his face says enough. "Oh, I didn't know..."

My face goes hot. "Um, Mr. Yearly, this is Lia. An old friend."

He nods. Calling Lia an old friend feels like betrayal. But Lia standing in front of me isn't real. Cannot be real. *Where, what, when* be damned, she's been gone so long I'd almost convinced myself I made her up.

But it's clear, as she tosses back her hair and bounds over to the old man, she is as real as the air I breathe. "Well, how do you do?"

His confusion melts for a beat, until he blinks a few times. "It's a pleasure," he says, going through the motions. She actually shakes his hand. I feel my smile before I realize it's there. She's still dramatic as ever.

"I was passing along when I saw Matthew."

"I see, well..."

She spins off, throwing a hand my way. "He was really after it, working so diligently. And I thought, I need to pull over and congratulate him on such effort."

Oh boy. Mr. Yearly looks to me for help, as though I've ever been able to stop Lia, who wanders back and forth before stopping abruptly and setting a hand on her hip. "He just talked that man out of going to Home Depot through sheer hard work and grit." She shakes her fist at my boss. "I'd give him a raise on the spot if I were you."

Mr. Yearly, blushing a bit, glances back to the doorway. "Yes, um, Matt, when you get a minute?"

"Be right there."

He takes another long glance at Lia. "And no friends on the dock, okay?"

"Yes, sir."

Lia salutes him.

The door shuts and Lia bows into laughter. I only watch her, trying to make sense of what is happening. Of what my boss must have been thinking. But nothing makes it past the runaway train of emotions blowing through the tracks of my brain.

I manage a shrug. "Well, some things never change."

She flips her hair up and pins me back with her eyes, biting her lip to break off her smile. "It's good to see you again."

"Yeah, you too."

I take another glance at the door when she takes my arm like it's no big deal. "And wow, what's going on? You're huge!"

"Oh." I'm caught between grabbing her hand and running down the road or shooing her off because if feels like I'm hallucinating. "Um, are you staying here?"

So much in that question, but Lia takes it in stride. "Well, it's a long story." Then, her eyes widening. "Hey, I'll tell you all about it. What time do you get off?"

Jen Yearly is picking me up at five. As in granddaughter of Mr. Yearly, owner of Yearly Farm and Supply. As in my girlfriend. And yet, I turn to the clock. Three forty-five. At three thirty-eight, my life was a set schedule. Predictable things like weight rooms, conditioning, work, and watching movies with Jen. Now, seven blurry minutes later, it all seems fake. Like someone else had been living it. Lia's here, and she wants to tell me all about it. I shrug. "I can be done in an hour."

Lia's hair is bit shorter but still with the natural highlights I remember so well. She tightropes the edge of the loading dock, setting her arms wide like she's on a balance beam. I blink. I rub my arm where she touched it. Because Lia is here. Now. She leaps off, and my heart explodes.

"See you then."

"Okay, yeah."

I watch her start off, still skipping like she's on a fairytale journey, when she turns around and waves real big like only Lia can. I wave back, heart pounding despite my better instincts. I worked hard to make the football team last year. And now, as a senior, things have begun to make sense.

Nothing makes sense. Sense is gone now as Lia climbs into a faded gold Honda, a clunker of a car with more dents than paint, missing hubcaps, and Georgia license plates. The driver's side brake light is out as she backs up and waves again. And I stand on the loading dock, looking at the clock, counting the minutes until I'll see her again.

Chapter 2

In the shop, Mr. Yearly is up front assisting an elderly lady with a birdfeeder. When he sees me, he waves me over. I try, and fail, to clear my mind of what's happening. Thankfully he doesn't ask about Lia on the loading dock when I approach.

"I have a gentleman out front who needs help with a wheelbarrow. He's been waiting for a bit."

Is Lia really here, in Maycomb? At work?

Mr. Yearly looks up, his eyes conveying annoyance. "Got it?"

"Yeah, sure." I start for the door when he calls me back.

"Matt?"

"Huh?"

I guess he wants me to explain why I'm on the loading dock hugging girls when I'm dating his granddaughter. But now the old lady is watching, and perhaps he senses this isn't the time. And while everything is weird at the store I might as well mention I need to leave fifteen minutes early. The old lady's face goes tight as she turns to Mr. Yearly for confirmation. He sets the birdfeeder on the counter.

"Today? I thought Jenny was picking you up?"

The old lady's head swivels to me. Birdfeeders. Wheelbarrows. Fertilizer. What's the use? Lia is here. All I can do is scratch my head. "Yeah, something's come up. I'll let Jen know."

With that, I walk out front, still in a daze.

Lia's car skids to a stop. The brakes wrench, and I'm waiting for a fender or door to fall off. She pulls her hair back and smiles. I climb in the car where there's an alarming amount of trash on the floorboard. The backseat is covered in clothes, shoes, books, a sleeping bag, and various appliances. I think I spot a blender.

She starts off, and I'm only hoping Mr. Yearly isn't watching from the windows. Lia doesn't say a word for the first couple of minutes, as I work to untangle the seatbelt until I catch her watching. Her face beams with fascination, like she's never seen a seatbelt in her life.

Lia.

Me.

Again.

Lia grips the steering wheel with both hands. "So, Mr. Higgins."

"Yeah," I say, clicking the seatbelt. I'm assuming she's only now heard the news of the old preacher's passing, back in spring. He'd been sick, we all knew it was coming, not that it made things any easier.

Reading my mind, Lia shakes her head. "No, I knew he'd passed. I feel terrible about missing his service. Let's just say it hasn't been the most stable of years."

"How'd you know? About his passing?" *Or where I work?* Again the questions rush my brain.

She turns to me, then the windshield, several times. I think she's about to cry before she shrugs it off. "Well, we talked, some."

I straighten up, blinking, and try to contain the jealousy in my voice. "What?"

Mr. Higgins' house sits at the end of my street along with five or six acres of woods. In those woods is a small pond where he baptized Lia that crazy summer, also where Lia and I canoed at midnight and kissed for the first time on the small dock. I realize I'm staring at her profile, down to where her neck meets her collarbone then back up to the curve of her lips.

Get a grip, Matt.

Lia glances at me, then down the road. We're headed in that direction, my street. Higgins' house. It's sat empty since his passing.

The occasional landscaping crew, an estate guy, not much else. My dad is terrified some big developer will snatch it up.

Finally, I spit it out. "You and Higgins were talking? All this time?"

Her hands come off the steering wheel. "You have your life, Matthew. Who am I to interfere?"

Lia and Mr. Higgins had a special bond, the way only two people who have lost someone close could share. Higgins had lost his wife, Lia her father. Now, she says she didn't want to interfere, as though it explains why she never called me but spoke to him *about* me.

I turn to the smeary window, away from her. My head is buzzing, tingling. If she didn't want to interfere, what's she doing now?

Sure enough, she turns down my street. I'm about to tell her I don't want to go home, to explain her to Mom, when she blurts out, "He left me his house."

Earth stops its rotation. Rocks slide off cliffs. The ocean rears itself back. A Tsunami is coming. "What?"

She shrugs. "The lawyers got in touch with me. Said it was all worked out. He didn't have much family left. He gave it to me. Well, some sort of trust thingy."

Words fail me. We pass the house where Lia and her mother lived in the basement that summer. It's been redone now, painted, new windows. Then we drive past my house, where I used to have a treehouse in the backyard where Lia slept a few times. She keeps driving. My mouth is still open.

Lia laughs. "I know, I know. I told him to give it to charity, but he was adamant. He said I would appreciate it. He said I was a good *treasure hunter,* whatever that means. I never thought he was actually going to leave it to me."

She pulls in the driveway to Higgins' house. *Her* house. She's still talking, but I'm having trouble taking in any new information. "He said he kept getting offers on it but turned them down. And you know what? A week ago some fancy realty firm called and offered me cash. Said it was double what the house is worth." She smiles. "You know how much fun it was telling them to pound sand? I thought it sounded like something he would have said, right?"

I'm not following. Can't follow. Lia creaks to a stop and parks the car. She looks me over with a smile. I've had dreams stranger than this, probably, but none of them are coming to mind.

She takes in the house. "I'm going to have to paint, though. If I remember correctly."

"Lia."

She turns to me with glittering eyes, the brightest eyes I've ever seen. Eyes that leave me struggling to focus. "You're moving back here?" I nod to the house. "You're going to *live* here?"

She sits back, arms extended as she grips the steering wheel. "Well, my mom is in jail, probably for the long haul." Her hands flop to her lap. "I've been sort of wandering around all summer, spring, winter...but yeah. I think so." She looks at the house again, then back to me. "Hey, let's walk down to the pond!"

Before I can answer, Lia is out of the car, tromping over the high grass that was Higgins' yard. I get out, slower, looking around. "Yeah, because this isn't weird at all."

The pond—where I chased after Lia at all hours. It was my first time sneaking out, first time doing a lot of things. And now, as she takes off without me, waltzing into the past, I don't have the heart to tell her how much everything has changed. Time machines don't exist. You don't leave someone, leave some*where* for three years and then come back like nothing's happened.

Do you?

I try not to think about what I'm doing. Or how I'm feeling. I look to Higgins' old house. Or what's going to happen. I look around once more, then jog to catch up with her.

"I can't believe this," she says as I catch up. She looks around, where everything is overgrown. Thickets where the trail used to be, briars and sticker bushes. She ducks and weaves and shoves branches out of the way. "Well, this might be the first course of action. Rebuilding our trail."

A branch lashes me in the chest. I have a girlfriend. Football practice starts next week. A life of my own worlds away from where I am now. I have a thousand reasons why this is no good, Lia coming here. *Living* here. Watching her crouch and weave through the limbs, smiling and laughing, I just can't think of one at the moment.

"Matthew, you should be ashamed of yourself, letting his happen. Higgins said you were doing well for yourself, with the job, and the..." she knocks her head back, looks me up and down, "football. But would it have killed you to maintain the path?"

"Well, sorry." I don't tell her I haven't been to the pond since she left. Had no reason to go to the pond after she left.

We plod deeper into the tangle of grass, weeds, bushes, and thorns. Lia is talking about all the things she needs to do. I'm thinking of all the memories I have in these woods, with her, how they too are overgrown and tangled up with time. And now, as we plunge into the past, it all comes rushing back so easily. Following Lia, her perfect legs, the whiffs of vanilla.

We arrive at the opening and she spreads her arms and exhales. I'm surprised to see little Geer Pond, where the dock still sits, a bit mangled and crooked. The water is still, a few ripples where the trees have dropped leaves. Otherwise it's how we left it.

Lia makes a run for it, and suddenly I'm thirteen again, calling after her. "Lia, don't."

She leaps to the dock and balances on an iffy slat of wood. I run to her. She looks off, wipes her hair back. "It's..." she shrugs. "It's how I remember it, mostly."

She looks around, then to me. My heart stops.

My first kiss. My first crush. My first realizations of the world outside of Maycomb. It stands beautifully before me, on the dock. Behind her the tiny pond is like a mirror, reflecting the trees around it, surrounded by bull frogs and bugs and chirping birds.

We don't say anything for a minute, as we take it in together. Then she turns to me. "So before we go any further, explain the football team thing. How in the world did that happen?"

I laugh, the tightness in my chest relaxing. I feel like a yo-yo, winding then releasing as she tiptoes out to the edge of the dock. I test my footing before I follow her. "Well, Maycomb High isn't exactly a powerhouse. Coach asked me to come out for the team last year."

She sits, kicks her feet out, and it's like she never left. I sit beside her, unsure how close until she nudges me on the arm. "Because you're so big."

"I guess. And, Lia, I don't know. I'm good at it. I didn't think I would be, but..."

Lia cuts her eyes to me. "You're good at a lot of things."

I'm caught in her charm, but it's fleeting, tangled in my annoyance. How could she know? How can she show up like this and pretend to know everything about me?

Before I can think much more on it, she skims the toe of her sneaker over the pond. I turn away, away from her eyes, from her brown legs, dark from sun, perfectly sculpted. Does Lia work out, go to a gym? I can't imagine it. But our arms touch, and I look down to the warmth of her tawny skin against my white arm. My old friends once made fun of Lia for being biracial. Looking at her now, the joke is on them. She's a walking magazine cover.

I look to her face. I need some answers. "So, where have you been? Can you at least tell me that?"

She nods, looks out past the pond. "Florida. Georgia. Here. There."

"Not here," I say before I can stop myself. She turns to me and I get to my feet, away from her. Because it's not fair, her questions about what I'm doing—football—while she's completely vague about everything she's been up to.

She watches me, then her gaze returns to the water. "Remember when I pushed you in?"

I roll my eyes as a smile returns. Of course. I remember every second with her, it's why this is so frustrating.

She gazes out at the pond as though it's a portal to the past. "Or when you ditched me on the canoe." She looks up at me, her eyes wide. "With that snake!"

I can't let her do this. She owes me an explanation. "Lia." I struggle to keep my voice from breaking. "It's been three years. Not a single letter or phone call. No Facebook message. Nothing. Now, you show up at work and we're at Greer Pond. And you're going to live here? It's a little jolting for me, okay?"

"I don't do Facebook, Matthew. Lame." Back to the pond.

"It's Matt." I throw my hands up. She turns to me and I recover with a shrug. "People call me Matt now."

She's on her feet in a flash. Her eyes narrow, and it's like she's only now seeing the pond for what it is—a tiny patch of water in a tiny middle of nowhere town. She fiddles with the ring on her pinkie finger before she takes a breath and nods. "Okay, look, I'm sorry I came. I just..."

I take a step back. Is this really happening?

"Lia, I'm sorry. I...it's a lot."

She pulls her hair back and sighs. "I know it is."

"No. I mean, are you okay? What's going on, with your car and everything?"

"Huh? Oh." She throws her hands out and laughs. It's a laugh that has haunted my dreams for the past three years. "Ha. Well, I've been camping a lot."

My mouth falls open. "Camping? Like, on the road? You're not in school?"

"Well, I sort of graduated early." She lowers her voice, swings her fist playfully. "Well, golly gee, I was going to get my GED!" Then, getting serious again. "But maybe, now, I can start fresh. Even as part of me feels bad, accepting the house and the money. But then again, Higgins really wanted me to have it. He insisted. The lawyers say it's all done, it's legit. They set up a trust or something. I..."

"Money?"

She kicks at the dock, peeks over to me. "Well, I don't know, there's some cryptic language. Anyway, Higgins didn't want to leave the house to the church, not after what happened, so..."

No surprise there. Maycomb Baptist had basically disowned him after he performed a same sex wedding. Lia and I were ushers. We danced together, found Higgins on this very dock later that night. And that was the last night I saw her. Until now.

She drops the act, takes a huge breath, and then she's someone else again. "Yeah, he was always after me to go to college." She laughs. "He still wants me to be a veterinarian. Or, *wanted* me to be, I should say."

I smile. She smiles. "Is that still what you want? Are you thinking about going to college?"

She gives me a shove and hops off the dock. "Don't look so surprised, Matthew—er, Matt. I'm actually quite smart."

Then I realize something, and the yo-yo in my chest winds all the way up and knots there. "Are you...will you go to Maycomb High this year?"

She cocks her head and smiles at me. "I haven't gotten that far yet. I don't know. Would that be okay with you?"

This day, this past hour, I can't put it in words. "Yeah, no. This is all so..."

I'm trying to find the words when Lia hops down and starts back the way we came. Done with it all. "Okay, well, I've got a lot to do."

Chapter 3

Of all the times I imagined Lia's return, it was never like this. I jog to catch up with her, climbing over a tree trunk, ducking branches, sticks snapping under my plodding steps. "Hey, I'm sorry. Can we start over?"

"A third time?" We're in the middle of the woods when she sets a finger to her chin. "Sure. Hi, uh, *Matt*. My mom is in jail. I took her car. I'm sort of just driving around, and well, I've been thinking about you for three years, and now I'm going to move into Mr. Higgins' old house. Thought I'd drop in." She throws her hands out. "There."

Then she's clomping off again.

"I've thought about you too."

She slows but doesn't stop.

"Every day."

Now she does stop, mid-duck under a thorn bush. She backs out, sets her hair back and tilts her head my way but never turns around.

I walk up to her. "So trust me, it isn't that I don't want to see you. It's more like, shock, I guess."

She turns around and smiles, and I catch myself wanting nothing more than to kiss her when I remember Jen, my girlfriend, who's probably looking for me right now. I rip out some undergrowth on the trail, looking for something to do with my hands.

"So, have you been living in your car?"

She bites her lip. "Not exactly *living* in it. I left last night. Had to get all our things from the apartment. It's not so bad."

I shake my head. She starts through the woods again, tangles of limbs and vines and a few felled trees until we get out to the clearing and I realize I'm laughing. Lia turns around, she's got burs on her shirt. "What?"

"Just...everything."

She looks me over. Then, with a smile, she dangles a key in my face. "Want to come inside?"

"Um..."

Her eyes widen. "To see the house! What did you think? Oh, Matthew—er, Matt. I can't believe you."

"I wasn't...no, I didn't mean it like that."

She starts for the house, laughing. "You really have become one of those football meatheads, haven't you?"

"Meatheads?"

She turns around and shoves me. "Yes."

We start up the hill, which isn't much of a hill as I remember, and now we're both laughing for no reason at all. I think we're both too confused to do anything else.

The old house still looks the same, although it needs a bit of sprucing where the boxwoods have grown out, and the gutters need a good cleaning. Lia asks about my parents. I tell her all about how my dad changed right before she left. How he came to Higgins' defense when few others would do so. How he began to listen to me, to realize I wasn't simply a miniature him.

"Higgins mentioned it."

We get to the porch, Lia looks over a rusted out chair. I shake my head. "Seriously. All this time I was wondering about you, and you and Higgins were like pen pals."

She reaches out and takes my hand. Electricity shoots through my limbs. "I told you, I didn't want to interfere."

My phone buzzes and Lia drops my hand. She looks to my pocket before she turns back to the door. "Besides, you clearly have your own life, anyway."

Had, I'm thinking. But I'm not doing that, not right now. Instead, I tell her more about that night, here at the wedding when my dad came down.

"Yeah, so my dad and I had this big fight after the wedding, when he yanked me home and I couldn't find you. Because you disappeared. Ever heard of saying goodbye, by the way?"

She glances at me. "I knew I was coming back." Her eyes fall to my mouth, then to my neck. She sucks in a breath.

"Oh, yeah." I pull the dog tag from beneath my shirt. "It's why you gave me this."

Her eyes are already welling when I reach back and remove the dog tag I've worn since she left it for me three years ago. The one people always ask about, the one that belonged to her father.

It jingles as I hand it to her. She holds it in her palm and looks it over, wipes her eyes, and then pulls me close and hugs me harder than anyone has ever hugged me.

When she pulls away she studies it again like it holds the secrets to the world. She told me once how much her father meant to her, before he died in Afghanistan. Now my chest feels cold. I feel naked without it.

She looks at me again, eyes wet and full. "So...you wore it? The whole time?"

"The whole time. Well, except..." I motion for her to turn around. She hands it to me and lifts her hair. I set it around her neck, my fingers lingering at her collarbone. I fasten the dog tag and she lets her hair down. When she turns back to me I'm lost. Because it always seemed like forever ago she left but now, here with her, it doesn't feel so long ago anymore. When she hugs me again, I feel myself being pulled toward her, closer. She lifts her head up and our noses are almost touching. I'm sunk.

"Hey, you two."

We jerk away like we've been shocked. Mr. Woods, the elderly neighbor, starts down the driveway like he's been hiding in the bushes. He must have heard us and thought we were trespassing. "You can't be down here." Then, cupping his hands to his face. "Matt? That you?"

"Oh, hi, Mr. Woods. We're just..."

Lia steps forward. "I'm the new owner."

He narrows his eyes. Lia, beaming, holds up the keys.

"Oh? Well…" He looks at the house as though it will answer all the questions clouding over his face. Then he simply nods to me and starts walking back down the driveway.

Lia scrunches up her face. "Well, that wasn't very neighborly."

Chapter 4

"Okay," she says, pausing at the door. "I haven't been inside since, before. But Sterling said I can do what I want with the contents, whatever that means. I sort of tuned him out when he was talking about utilities and property taxes and blah blah blah."

"Lia, that's important."

She nods. "Yeah, he said that too."

"Now, who's Sterling?"

"The lawyer guy."

When we walk into the living room, a familiar, musty scent hits my nose. Lia starts singing. *"Memories, in the corner of my mind."*

His old record player. A clock on the mantel ticks off the time—the wrong time. His reading glasses and a notepad by the sitting chair. It's like he's in the other room.

Lia, who was singing and joking only moments ago, goes quiet. Her eyes are shiny with tears all over again. I'm not even thinking about it as I set my arm around her and she leans into me with a weepy giggle. "I'm only a few steps in and I'm already crying."

We make it to the kitchen, where Lia helped the preacher with the wedding officiating. The cabinets are still filled with his plates, cups, glasses. Mr. Higgins' mason jars take up the corner. Stuff is everywhere.

"So there was no family?"

Lia finds a tissue. "Nope. Seriously. Matt, I refused this every time he brought it up. The first time the lawyers spoke to me they acted like I was up to something." She picks up the phone on the wall and sets it to her ear. Her eyes go wide then she sets it back on the hanger thing. "Trust me, I didn't ask him for any of this."

"No, I know."

She fingers the dog tag, like it was never gone. Again I remind myself about Jen. Jen is sweet and nice and pretty, and my parents are crazy about her. So what am I doing? I've abandoned the present and now I'm sitting with Lia, who launches into a story about a truck stop in Marietta, Georgia.

Technically, I'm not doing anything *wrong*—besides my thoughts, feelings, emotions—I'm simply catching up with an old friend. At least that's what I'm telling myself when my phone buzzes for the tenth time in an hour, as though to urge me to take my thoughts more seriously.

Lia glances my way. "Uh oh."

I reach into my pocket and silence the phone. "Uh oh, what?"

"Matthew, um, Matt. I'm sure you have a girlfriend." She gestures at me with her hand. "Being that you're Mr. Muscle these days and on the football team. Is she upset?"

"I'm not Mr.... No. No one's upset."

My phone buzzes again. I pull the phone from my pocket as though to show her I'm not worried. This time it's a text from Mom.

Jen is here.

Three words wrestle me back to reality. And Lia sees it in my eyes. I smile. "It's my mom. Hey, I've got to run home, but I can be back soon, to help with..." I look around the room. "Whatever you need."

She nods with a smile. I start for the door.

"Matt?"

I stop.

She holds up the dog tag. "Thank you. I can't tell you what it means to me. That you kept this."

I smile. "Yeah. Of course. And...you can call me Matthew."

She looks up, and we stare at each other in the quiet house. My phone buzzes again, reminding me there are other people in the world. I nod to the box of a television on the floor. "Well, I'll be back okay, don't go trying to move furniture without me."

She laughs. "Okay, I won't."

I speed walk up the street, realizing I haven't walked up my own street in a long, long time. A rush of excitement falls over me, and I try to hold it together, but I'm flushed and floating, thinking about Lia's smile in the room and still dizzy from the thought of her living in Mr. Higgins' house with the antiques and rotary phone and vinyl records.

It's too weird, weird enough for Jen and my mom to exchange looks as soon as I sweep through the door. I slow myself down, take a breath, and attempt to appear like a rational human being.

I fail.

Mom and Jen stand up from the table. Mom shoots me a quick look I don't have time to decipher because Jen walks up to me. "Matt. Are you okay?"

Jen Yearly and I got to know each other last year when we partnered up in chemistry class. She's the one who got me the job at Yearly Farm and Supply, the job I just ditched early. She's in the National Honor Society and more recently received an acceptance letter to UNC Greensboro offering a partial soccer scholarship.

Blonde and pretty, Jen is popular, liked by everyone. We get along well, even though sometimes it seems like we're struggling with what to talk about. When that happens we usually fall back on sports.

"Matt?"

Wait. What was the question? Oh yes, am I okay? *Yeah, sure. I'm okay.* Okay for someone whose dreams have barged into his real life without an appointment or warning. Jen looks me up and down, to the hitchhikers on my pant legs, the bits of branches still caught in my shirt.

"What in the world have you been doing? I tried to call," she says, as though I didn't know that.

Mom, in the kitchen, pretends to be interested with some junk mail at the table. I realize now that if I was trying to downplay things, I've failed miserably. I start with the truth—some of it. "I was down at Higgins' place." I start for the fridge because my mouth is dry.

Mom doesn't help me out when she suddenly stops and looks at me. "Oh?"

"Yeah, um, thing is," I laugh, only it's not my laugh, it's someone else's squeaky high pitched laugh that only sounds stranger when I make myself stop. "Um, well, see, an old friend is back in town and she..."

And still, up until now I might have had a chance. Things were weird but manageable. But the "she" coming out of my mouth hits the room like a bomb.

Jen, still smiling, tilts her head. "She? Wait. Old friend. The one you told me about? Lia?"

One time, over summer, we were camping with friends when we started talking about first loves. Jen was being cute like I was her first love, and then I opened my mouth and told her about Lia—a lot about Lia. Seeing her reaction now, waaayyy too much about Lia.

Jen's still looking me over, and again Mom does me no favors when she drops a pan. "*Lia's* here? In Maycomb?"

And it's the snowflake that starts the avalanche. Jen's little smile twitches, and even as she's still faking that she's happy, Mom's not faking that she isn't giddy, and I have twigs in my hair from romping around in Preacher Higgins'—nope, scratch that—*Lia's* property, and Mom and Jen are standing in front of me and it's like I'm screaming how badly I need to bust out the door and run back down there.

Slowly I nod. Jen's face does more acrobatics. A flash of anger before she attempts to recover. Then disappointment, followed by something else, stubbornness, maybe?

Jen looks over my shoulder, like Lia is on the porch. "Where is she? Can I meet her?"

"Oh, um, right." Now Mom's looking past me, and I check over my shoulder just in case Lia really is on the porch. She's not. "Well, there's more to the story. And yes, of course, just, well..." I stop, wondering what I'm saying. "Um, Jen. I kind of need to help her with some stuff."

This is met with wide eyes from both Mom and Jen.

Mom breaks it off. "Is Lia okay?"

"Yeah, she's down at Mr. Higgins' house. Well, her house. It's—"

"*What?*" they say in unison.

"Yeah, Mr. Higgins left her his house."

"Why?" Jen says, her voice cracking. Her face is balled up in confusion. "I heard he was kind of loopy towards the end, acting strange and…" she shakes off the thought. "Why would he give her *his house?*"

I shrug. "He had no family. They were really close." I look at Mom, who's now flushed as I must be. It's almost as if she wants to shoot out the door and bolt down there as badly as I do.

Mom finally notices Jen's irritation and makes an excuse to leave us alone. "Well, I need to check on the laundry."

Once she's gone, Jen walks to the window, her fingers fiddling. "Matt, you're acting strange."

"I know, I'm sorry, it's well, it's all kind of crazy." I laugh.

But Jen doesn't laugh. She turns suddenly. "We're still going to the movie, right?"

The movie. What movie? How could I possibly go sit in a dark room and watch a movie right now? Knowing Lia is down there and three years have gone by and I'm terrified she's going to leave again.

And then it hits me all over again. Maycomb High. What will I do if Lia really sticks around and enrolls in school?

I'm lost in that thought, so I don't even realize Jen has left the window and stands in front of me, asking me something. "Matt. Hello?"

"Sorry, what?"

She looks at me for a minute.

I shake my head. "Jen, I can't go to the movie tonight."

She stares at me. "I don't–" A big sigh. "What's happening, Matt?"

"Nothing. Nothing is happening." *So much is happening.* "I just, I need to think about some things."

The shock comes and goes quickly. A flash sparks in her eyes as she gathers her things, nodding. We've been going out since prom last year, and I've never heard her voice this sharp. She gathers her bag off the couch. "You do that, Matt. Go think about some things and let me know what you come up with."

Chapter 5

Jen storms out, throws her car in gear, and tears down the street, out of the neighborhood.

Mom returns. "That didn't sound like it went great."

"You were listening?"

"So, Lia's back. What in the world, about Mr. Higgins' place?"

"I know." I tell her about the lawyers, about the keys. I tell Mom I'm going back down there to help, and she offers to come down in a bit with a casserole.

I laugh. Mom and her casseroles.

When I return to Higgins' place forty-five minutes later, Lia has made zero progress. In fact, things might be worse. She's in tears, sitting on the floor, her legs tucked beneath her, looking through old photo albums.

"Are you okay?"

"It's so sweet." She holds up a black and white photo from a wedding album, a young Preacher Higgins and his pretty wife, Jolene. She pats the place beside her and I sit. I'd figured she'd have me moving things around. Instead she spreads out the album. "They were so in love."

I look around. The house is a mess of boxes and letters and photos. Anyone else would have shoved this stuff into a dumpster. Maybe this is why the old man chose Lia. He knew she'd appreciate his keepsakes, that she'd take care of everything.

She lets out a misty gust. "Sorry. I didn't get much of anything done. I think I made it worse."

I'm about to make a joke about it when she adds, "Hey, you want to get something to eat? There's nothing but ketchup in the fridge."

My first thought goes to Mom and her casserole, but then I imagine Mom rushing in and making everything weird and I'm not ready for all of that yet. Instead, I think about Lia and me in the car, getting away from everyone. "Yeah, I know just the place."

Lia goes out to her car to get a change of clothes. I send Mom a text, and she sends me a frowning emoticon. I offer to drive and we begin the hike up the street to my house. I feel the stares from every window as Lia skips along. It's new but familiar all at the same time.

"So, I think Mr. Higgins left a treasure."

I glance at her sideways. With Lia, it's impossible to tell if she's serious or has cooked up some wild concoction in her mind. "Treasure?"

"Yeah, it started when he referred to some trust 'on the property,' but then I found a note. Well, lots of notes. And some," she wiggles her eyebrows, "some I think are clues."

My feet drag to a stop. "Are you being for real?"

She turns to me and we're standing in the middle of the street. She holds her hand to her heart. "How could you ask such a thing?"

"Well, what do you mean, a 'note'?" I throw my hands out. "A 'treasure'?"

She crosses her arms over her chest. "I'll show it to you later."

"Why would he bury a treasure?"

Lia rolls her eyes. "You know what, forget it. It's just a hunch. It might be nothing. You keep saying treasure like you're making fun of me."

"You said *treasure* first."

She smirks at me. I bust out laughing and she does the same. We start up the street again. As soon as we get to my driveway I try to warn Lia. "You know my mom wants to see you."

Before she can answer, Mom busts out of the house, arms out and coming in like she's going to make a tackle. "I don't believe it," she gushes.

I roll my eyes as Mom and Lia hug in the yard.

"Hi, Mrs. Crosby."

Mom pulls away, grabs Lia's hands, and takes her in. "Wow, I can't believe it."

Lia kicks at a rock.

I try to intervene. "Mom."

Mom ignores me. "I'm making you a casserole. Matt says you're staying down the street?"

Lia glances at me, then nods. "Yeah, it's kind of crazy. I'm just getting settled."

"Oh well, this is... And school, will you go to—"

"Mom!"

"What?"

Lia looks over the house and Mom looks at me and mouths. "Wow!"

I pretend I have no idea what she means. "We're going out to Porter Grill," I say.

Mom scrunches up her brow. "All the way out there?"

I shrug.

Mom takes the hint. "Okay. Well Lia, whatever you need in the meantime."

I get Mom inside and go to find the car keys when she stops me. "Matt."

"Huh?" I say, still looking for the keys.

Mom picks them up from the table, right in front of me. "I'm a little concerned though."

She's worried.

"Why?" I watch Lia in the yard. Mom comes up behind me.

"About you and Jen. You're...well, this is all unexpected and..." She lowers her voice even though no one's in the room. "Matt, she's..." Mom gestures toward the window. "She's beautiful."

I shake her off and go for the door. "Lia is a friend, Mom. That's all. I'm not doing anything wrong." Mom looks at me and I try to hold her gaze but can't, not even for a second. "Look, I have to go. We'll be back later."

Mom closes her eyes with her smile. "Okay."

I walk outside and find Lia around the side of the house. My heart drops, because I know what's coming.

"Where's the treehouse?"

"Huh? Oh, we tore it down."

She turns to me, then back to the two trees that once held the treehouse where we spent so much time. Suddenly I feel terrible. "It was rotting and…"

I remember that day, thinking I would feel better after it was gone. I didn't, and Dad chuckled and asked if I was okay. Of course he had no idea that Lia had slept there when she was having problems at home, or about all the talks we'd had in there. He just saw that it was falling apart.

Lia nods and looks at the trees one more time. Then, with a smile, she's over it. "Okay, where to?"

It's true, Porter Grille is *all the way out there*, far away from town. Not like I'm avoiding anything. Maybe I just want a great steak and I'm willing to drive fifteen miles out to Cara County.

Lia doesn't say much for a while, until we're out on the two lane road and she turns to me, suddenly. "Am I messing things up, like, with your girlfriend, Jackie?"

Her arms are covered in goosebumps. I turn down the AC. Again, I notice the dog tag on her neck and my hand instinctively goes to my own. I laugh off her question. Mr. Casual and all. "It's Jen. And no. She's fine."

Lia's eyes linger on me for a moment, then she hops up straighter and starts playing with the radio. She finds an oldies station and leaves it. "So tell me, Matthew. What do you like to do these days? Football? Work? Hang with Jen."

"Oh, well, yeah mostly. Football is fun. Practice is about to start, so…"

"What did you do all summer? Go on any trips, adventures?"

"What, like treasure hunts?"

She sticks her tongue out at me.

"Well, I went to the beach. And..."

She nods. "Okay, that's fun. What else?"

What does she want me to say? *Adventures?* I spent the summer with Jen, going to movies and hanging out at her house. Helping her dad fix up one of his rental properties. Now, looking over at her sort of bobbing along to music my grandparents listen to, her legs bouncing, smooth and screaming for me to stare at them, I feel a bit underwhelming.

"I didn't do much. Conditioning and stuff."

She smiles, as though trying to make me feel better. "Okay, and I can see it's paid off."

"And you? You just been driving around?"

"Pretty much. I did some of the Appalachian Trail. Met this group called the Hyper Hikers. They were basically running the entire trail. Like, all the way up the coast. It was crazy. I didn't last long."

That explains her toned appearance. I laugh. "And you ran with them?"

She shakes her head. "Only the downhill parts."

I stare at her, laughing harder than I can remember laughing in a while. "You nut. You just picked up and started running with these random strangers?"

She throws her arms up. "Why not? It was fun. Until I fell." She kicks her leg out to show me a small scar on her knee. "That sucked. They were nice though, they took care of me."

I catch myself before I warn her about meeting up with strangers. I picture Lia, cutoff jeans and sandals, meeting up with random hikers and hanging out. Them taking care of her. Who does that? Lia does.

I pull in to Porter Grill and Lia looks around wildly. The gravel parking lot is packed, and the big neon sign rains light down on the shiny SUV hoods. She shimmies back in her seat. "Well ain't this fancy?"

"Yeah."

It's a twenty minute wait for a table. Mom's words echo in my head. But so what? Lia's pretty. There's no rule that says we can't be friends. And yeah, people are watching her, but that's probably because she's tossing peanuts in the air and nearly diving to catch them in her mouth. It all comes back fast, her dining manners, or lack of dining manners. A baby watches her with a huge smile. I tell myself she's a regular girl. This is not a date. Jen will get over it.

Lia turns to me, eyes full of mischief. "Hey, you know what I was thinking about?"

"Never."

"Ha. I was thinking about that time we caught Mr. Higgins down at the pond. Remember that?"

How could I not? Sneaking out of my house, meeting up with Lia so she could lead me down to the small pond, where, across the water, Mr. Higgins took off his robe like he was going skinny dipping.

Soon, we're cracking up, reliving old times, when my little pager buzzes. We're folded over, going on about poor Preacher Higgins, when Lia takes my arm to keep from face planting on the floor. Then I hear my name.

"Matt?"

Zap. I'm sucked out of the play pretend world of Lia and into my real life.

"Oh, um, hey, Courtney."

Of course, fifteen miles outside of town, I find Courtney Jenkins, one of Jen's soccer teammates. She makes no effort to hide her blatant staring at Lia, before she moves on to me with arched eyebrows. "Hi," she says, clearly waiting for an explanation.

Lia unloops her arm from mine and squeals. "Oh, great. I'm sooo hungry. Do you know if there's free bread?"

Courtney's lips part. She looks at me again, eyes widening, mouth open. I shrug.

"Um, right this way."

It isn't until we take our table, at a crowded steakhouse, as I'm trying to come up with something to say to Courtney, that Lia informs me she is a vegetarian. Two menus slap the table and Courtney marches off. I ask Lia why she didn't tell me that before, and she said I'd looked too excited about choosing the restaurant.

Between the bread and the two salads, she makes it work. She also gets a bowl of mac and cheese and cleans that up. I eat a steak, baked potato, and then we split an ice cream sundae.

If she notices the way Courtney looks at her, or speaks to me, she doesn't say anything. Instead she launches into a story about how she talked some people into letting her join them on a hot air balloon ride in North Carolina.

It's at some point, as Lia, with chocolate on the corner of her mouth, leans over the table to ask if I want to see the note of what might be, could be, a treasure map, I realize maybe my mom was right. How's this going to work?

It's not. That's how.

I PULL UP TO HIGGINS' house, between the holly bushes that line the driveway. Lia stretches and yawns, and I put the car in park. Lia does a spot-on impression of a guy at the restaurant making a fuss about his bill.

"I'm not paying for your mistake, that's that," she says in a perfect drawl.

I'm laughing, but I can't help myself. "I always thought you would have gone into theater."

She cocks her head, mocking offense. "Life is my theater, Matthew, er, *Matt*."

"I told you to call me Matthew, it's fine."

"Well, if *Matt* is your name, it's fine. It's a new you."

"It's not that new, Lia."

She glances up to me, then nods. "Yeah, I guess not. Hey, take a walk? You're supposed to be able to see the Space Station tonight."

I shake my head. "What? How do you even…okay, sure."

We fight through the trail to get to the pond, where we take the dock and her hands instinctively go to the dog tag.

"So what's your plan? With your mom and all?" I ask.

She sits and stares up at the sky as though daring it to dazzle her. A few sighs, and she shrugs. "I don't know. I think she's going to be there a while this time. We haven't spoken in months."

I picture Lia the vagabond, up and down the coast, going out west, farther away, how I might never see her again. Then she sets her head on my arm, and we stare at the sky, looking for lights. And for a while I forget about what happened with work, Jen, and everything else in the hours since Lia's return.

When I walk her back to the house, she stops at the porch and twirls. "Well, that was fun. Thanks for dinner. You didn't have to pay—well, I suppose you did because I don't have any money."

"About that, how are you going to live here?"

"Oh," she says. "Sterling said there's money in the trust for utilities and what not. And then there's the treasure. Or I'll get a job."

I try to imagine Lia with a job. Waitressing? That's a laugh. She's much more qualified for treasure hunting.

We linger for a bit. She smiles at me, and I'm afraid to let her go. She takes one more look to the sky when my phone buzzes. Lia breaks away. "Well, I'll let you get that."

"Oh, yeah, okay. Are you sure you're okay, here by yourself? Wait, that's not what I meant exactly, but…"

She chuckles. "Yeah, I'll be fine."

"I can come down tomorrow and help, if you'd like."

"That would be great." She opens the screen door. "Thanks again, Matthew."

"Yeah, no problem. Goodnight."

"Goodnight."

She screen door shuts. I walk down the path to the car. And I'm sitting in the driver's seat, when I look up and see her still in the light of the porch. She gives me a little wave, then slowly closes the door, leaving me alone with the sky to guess about space stations and old photos, treasure maps.

My phone buzzes again. I turn the car around and head home.

Chapter 6

I find Mom in the den, reading a paperback. She sets it on her knee as I sit down beside her.

"Dad working late again?"

She nods. "Well, how did it go?"

I stretch and try to blink out of the daze that was this afternoon. "We went out to Porter Grill." I throw my hands up. "One of Jen's friends is a hostess."

"Oh, that's awkward."

"Yeah, I'm getting ready to call Jen, she's blowing me up." Mom's smile remains neutral. I look off. "This is crazy. Lia just showed up at work. I thought it was a dream."

Mom nods, listening but not really.

I turn to her. "This is the part where you give me great advice."

She removes her reading glasses, rubs her eyes. "Matt, I know how much she meant to you." She ducks her head to get my attention. "Means to you still?"

I cock my head. "But?"

She gives me the mom look, the don't-even-try-it look. "Matt, one look at you earlier, and...well, you were almost swirly-eyed. I just don't want... I think you need to be honest with Jen."

I jerk away from her. "I was. I am. I'm not doing anything wrong. Is it so bad for me to catch up with a friend?"

"Of course not. Is that what you're doing? Is Lia an old friend, or something else entirely?"

Something else entirely sounds about right. I run a hand through my hair. I've always been better at talking to my mom than my dad. "I don't know. It doesn't seem real. It took me forever to get over her, and now I've got my own life and everything was figured out. And then, she appears. She moves into Higgins' house? What the hell?"

Mom grimaces at my choice of words. "I wish I had an easier answer for you. I can't believe she's going to live there all by herself. Although, if any seventeen-year-old can, it's her."

I nod.

She looks closer at me, gesturing to her neck. "The dog tag."

I set my hand to my chest. "Yeah, I gave it back to her."

Mom smiles. "I'm sure that made her happy."

"Yeah."

She sets her hand on my back. "Matt. My advice to you is, be honest with yourself. And to Jen. She deserves that much."

I turn back to her. "Okay, thanks."

In the kitchen, I glance at the pictures on the fridge. There's one of Jen and me—several of Jen and me—why do I feel bad about it? Is it because the guy in the picture is more of an actor than real? Some guy playing the role of high school jock? I feel like a fraud.

I head to my room and call Jen. She picks up on the first ring but doesn't say hello, just breathes into the phone.

"Hello?" It's a dumb thing to say, but I'm not exactly good at talking to someone panting on the other end.

"Jen?"

More breathing.

"Jen, look, about today."

Breathing still.

"Jen, I'm sorry. Look, Lia is an old friend, I told you that, but we were close and it's—"

"Close? You ditched me to go hang out with some other girl, and I'm supposed to be okay with it? With you taking her to Porter Grill, on a freaking date?"

I knew she'd hear about it from Courtney, just not so fast. "We were just catching up." In my head I hear Lia making a corny ketchup joke. I hold my laughter when I hear crying on the other end.

"And don't think I didn't hear all about it."

"Um, okay, anyway, nothing's going on. We're simply hanging out. In fact, you should meet her. Maybe tomorrow, I have to help her—"

"Wait, what? You're going there tomorrow?" The anger in her voice throws me off. I've never heard Jen get angry at all. Now she sounds like she wants to kill me.

"I said I'd help her unpack. And there's this note..." I actually laugh. "A treasure map she thinks, but..."

"What?" she screams.

"Jen, look, I..."

I look down at the phone.

Call ended.

I call her back, ready to plead with her voicemail, but she picks up.

"Do *not* call me anymore. I can't believe you, Matt."

"Jen, what? I'm telling you the truth."

"You are *not*." Her voice breaks. "Courtney said you were basically drooling at the table. Courtney said the whole restaurant could tell you were in love with her."

She's crying hard now, and I feel like a scumbag because there's no way I'm not going down there tomorrow. Not because I'm in love with Lia, but because she's an old friend, and I can't make myself not want to go down there and hunt for treasure.

"Jen, that's ridiculous."

"Tell me you don't care about her."

"What?" I'm still thinking about Courtney. I don't look at Lia like that, do I? "Jen, of course I care about her, she's a friend."

"Tell me you don't have other kinds of feelings for her."

The past. The summer. The woods. The pond. Following Lia down a path without any idea what might happen next... Adventure...

"Matt."

"Huh?"

"You know what, Matt? You are an asshole."

I shake my head. "Jen."
Call ended.

Chapter 7

Saturday morning I wake up to Dad shuffling around the kitchen. It's a bit after seven—late by his standards—and I'm smiling as I stretch, blinking into the sun streaming through my blinds. Then it hits me like a jolt of electricity. Lia is down the street.

It wasn't a dream. She's here.

I grab a box of cereal, the milk, bowl, and spoon and join Dad at the table.

"Good morning," Dad says with a yawn.

Dad's gone gray at the temples. Bags stretch under his eyes. I really wish he'd leave the jail where he works as a correctional officer, but I think he feels vested. He's been there nearly twenty years, only a few more until retirement. Although I'm not sure what he'd do with himself then.

"Hey, Dad."

"How was work yesterday?"

I stop mid milk pour. "Oh, um, good."

"Yeah?" He eyes me carefully.

Okay, so Mom told him. I sigh. "So you heard about Lia."

He nods. "I cannot believe Higgins left her that property."

My dad's biggest fear is that all the land will get developed by an apartment complex. Still, it's annoying this is the first thing he wants to talk about. "Dad, she's not going to sell it."

He shakes his head. "Wait until the offers roll in."

"They have. She told them to beat it. I think Higgins left it to her because he knew she *wouldn't* sell. Either way, she needs some help down there. There's some water damage in the living room. And it needs some serious remodeling."

Dad arches an eyebrow.

I shake my head. "What?"

"You've already been inside." His chair groans as he sits back, clasps his hands. "I won't say it."

I roll my eyes. My cereal's getting soggy. "Jen. I know, she isn't happy about it. But it's not like that."

"Your mother said she's gorgeous."

I shrug. "I didn't notice."

"Right." Dad crosses his arms, his massive forearms invading my space. "Look, promise me you won't lose your mind over this, okay? You've worked so hard to get where you are. You're on your way to a scholarship, Matt."

"I know, I know."

"You know. And still you're about to ditch conditioning and go down there, aren't you?"

Jen and I run every weekend. Well, she runs me to death and we call it conditioning. I look at him with a little smile on my face. "I was thinking about it."

He takes a sip of his coffee. It's not the reaction I was expecting, and it throws me off. The next thing I know I'm pleading with him. "Dad, I need to help her get settled in, that's all."

"Is it? What about work?"

"I'm off today." *And maybe forever once Mr. Yearly talks to his granddaughter.*

"And Jen?"

I look away but catch Dad as he rolls his neck, cracking it all the way down. "Just try to keep a level head, okay son? I trust you, but this, this isn't... I don't know."

That makes two of us.

I GET DOWN TO HIGGINS' place around ten, where the horns of big band music drift from the open windows. The front door is wide open. I knock on the screen door. Nothing. Maybe the music is too loud. "Hello?"

Still nothing. I let myself in. "Lia?"

A record spins on the polished floor model; I walk over to it, about to turn it down when I catch movement in the corner of my eye. I spin, and Lia and I both jump and scream at the same time. She recovers with a laugh. But seeing how she's only wearing a bra and underwear, a towel in her hand, I quickly turn my head. "Oh, I'm sorry."

She pads across the floor and turns down the volume. I peek over to her. She's towel drying her hair. "Oh my gosh you scared me!"

Still in bra and panties. Purple bra, white panties. I set my gaze on the floor, although she doesn't seem at all worried about it.

I talk to the fireplace. "I'm sorry, I can... I didn't know you were...well..."

"Oh." Lia throws her hand up.

I turn slightly.

Lia looks down, like she only now realizes. "Oh, sorry. I'll go get dressed." She smiles. "I have to show you something."

I'm not sure how to react to that, so I sink into the couch, my cheeks flushed and my heart racing. Someone yodels about Chattanooga.

A few minutes later Lia reappears, this time fully clothed in a t-shirt and cut offs, hopping on one foot. "Do you know how good a shower feels after you've stayed up all night cleaning?"

I keep my eyes down.

Lia wanders over to the record player and clicks a button. The record slows to a stop. "Okay, how cool is that?" she says.

I keep my head bowed.

"Matthew. Are you there?"

I nod at the door. "Yeah, look, I'm really sorry about walking in like that."

She looks at the door. The sun hits her face, and it's like she's glowing. "Oh. It's okay." She laughs. "Really, what's the difference? Bathing suit, bra, same thing, right?"

"Um, sure."

She starts hopping again, like a nut, her wet hair flopping and her barefoot thumping the floor. Then she stops hopping and stares at me for a moment, and I'm still feeling weird when she lights up. "Oh, yeah. You have to see this. Come on!"

Before I can answer she snatches my hand and yanks me through the kitchen and down the steps to the basement, where it's more of the same: piles of boxes, papers, notes, and records. The must and mildew collide with Lia's fresh clean shower scent. And Dad would have a fit if he saw the corrosion on the hot water heater.

She leads me through Mr. Higgins' woodshop and out the backdoor where she stops at the garage, setting her hands on her hips. "Okay, are you ready?"

"I think so," I say, confused. "Um, I've been in the garage before. Remember? I used to cut his grass on the riding mower?"

She pulls her hair back with both hands. Her eyes hold a devilish gleam. "Yes, but I'm sure you weren't paying attention."

"To the mower?"

"Okay," she says, ignoring me. She clicks a button and the left door shudders and lifts, and she's squealing and hopping in place as it opens.

But she's right, I'd never been in through the other bay door, because something's in the way, something covered in the dusty green canvas she's pointing to. I spot a bit of chrome beneath the tarp.

Her smile grows. "I didn't take it off all the way, I was waiting for you."

Waiting for me. My heart gallops, and I remind myself of what Dad said about Jen. I focus on the car, the shine of the chrome peeking out. "Wow, looks fancy, whatever it is."

The bay door bangs to a stop. Lia takes both my hands. "Yeah, it's fancy. It's a 1962 Chrysler Newport."

"Wow." I scratch my head. "Wait, um, how do you know that?"

Lia drops my hands and smiles. "I told you I stayed up all night. Anyway, so I found a note in a drawer, with a set of keys and a title."

I take a step toward the tarp.

Lia follows me. "Say what you want about Higgins, he was meticulous. So I found all this stuff, but it was dark and I wanted to wait for you. You're welcome, by the way. So I grabbed my phone." She looks around, whispering. "I'm leeching on Mr. Wood's WIFI, shh."

"Lia, the car."

"Oh, right. So I got on Google. Did you know there are only two-hundred-sixty-two of these left?"

"Oh."

"Yeah, *oh*." She pulls out a ring with two keys on it and shakes them in my face. "So this morning, I ran back here and found this." She leaps past me to the tarp. "Well come on, let's see what we've got."

Slowly we peel the tarp back. And what we find is a white convertible Chrysler, in mint condition, with fat whitewall tires and a big shiny grill, the headlights angling down at a mean slant.

Lia stands back and admires the car. Not a dent or scratch. In fact, minus a tiny chip-sized splotch of rust in the back, it's showroom ready. Red interior. And while I should be looking at the car, I'm stuck on Lia. "Do you think this is the treasure?"

She cuts her eyes to me. "No. This is not the treasure. This is my new ride."

It takes a while, but we manage to dig out some jumper cables. Lia pulls the Honda around and parks in front of the Chrysler and we try to jumpstart it. Nothing.

We try again, then again, until Lia's smile fades and she stops poking her head out of the Honda asking if we should try again now.

I'm sweating, covered in grease and oil but not about to give up. And then, something comes to mind. "Hey, I know someone who can get this car started."

My dad's a car guy, and nothing gets him going like working

under the hood. I call him up, and all it takes is the mention of an antique car in the garage for him to start asking questions. I tell him what I can, and he abandons his weekend yardwork and grabs his tools. Then Mom insists on coming too, which means twenty minutes later all four of us are standing around the garage. Dad with an awkward greeting to Lia. Mom and Lia hugging each other again like they hadn't just gotten reacquainted yesterday.

Dad directs me to get behind the car. I wade through all the junk in the garage to push as he puts it in neutral. We manage to coast the old beast out of the garage where Dad circles it, whistling and muttering to himself.

He pops the hood and whistles again. "This has been completely restored at some point."

Lia looks to me. I shrug.

Finally, Dad turns to Lia. "This is something else."

She nods. "I know, right?"

"No, it's... I don't have an exact figure, but this car, this would fetch a good price."

"Oh," Lia says. "That's cool."

Dad shakes his head and turns to her to emphasize the point. "I'm talking possibly fifteen, twenty-thousand dollar range. Maybe more."

We wait for Lia to celebrate, like she's won the lottery. A house, a car. She's a seventeen-year-old dropout who can sell it all and start fresh. Instead, she blinks in the sun and runs a hand over the hood. "But I don't want it to fetch a good price, I want to drive it. Do you think you can get it to run?"

Dad's eyes go wide. A slow grin spreads across his face, and he laughs like a kid. He looks at the car, then to me. "You bet I can. Matt, grab my toolbox."

Chapter 8

While Dad and I dive in, Mom and Lia disappear in the house for a while. After a thorough inspection Dad suggests we make a run to the auto shop.

On the way, he looks at me. "Can I say something about it?"

"The car?"

He shoots me a look. "Matt. I get it, okay?"

I squirm in my seat.

He laughs. "I won't say too much, but she's...you know, I can see why... Look, try and let Jen down easy, okay? She's a sweet girl."

"Dad, I'm not...that's not what this is about."

Dad levels a gaze on me.

I look out the window and sigh. "I don't know."

At the auto store, my dad speed-walks through the aisles, talking to himself in a language only employees and car buffs would understand. We fill a cart with all sorts of sprays, oils, plugs, hoses, and whatever else.

We run into some older guys who want to talk football. We go through the motions. Dad played in high school and the team went to states. Now Maycomb is back, and it's going to be a good season. *You boys are going to get it done this year.* All that. Finally, they ask Dad what he's working on.

Dad pats me on the back. "Oh, just helping out a neighbor."

Back at the car, Dad removes the spark plugs, oils the ports. We drag out an air compressor and get some air in the tires. Then we drop a new battery in, and the car cranks but doesn't quite turn over. With a string of curse words, Dad grabs a can of spray and gets back to the engine.

Roughly ten minutes and several expletives later, he tells me to turn the key.

The Chrysler sputters to life. Dad tells me to give it gas, more gas. The whole car rocks as the engine catches and roars. Dad pumps his fist. "Yeah!"

I do the same, still gunning the gas because it's idling rough. I honk the horn a few times before Lia comes running outside wearing old timey sunglasses and a silk scarf as she launches into my dad for a hug. Dad holds his oil stained hands out and away from her, and I'm laughing as he looks to me for help.

She breaks away from Dad. "Okay, we have to take a ride."

"Well, you need tags, those are expired, and..." he tosses the towel to the side. "Oh, screw it. I suppose a trip around the block won't hurt."

I stand in disbelief as Lia lets out another squeal. She leaps over the door and basically into my lap. I slide over and Lia fiddles with the seat. Mom stands next to Dad.

"Well, are you guys coming?" Lia looks to them, her magic spreading through us, even working on my dad, who smiles at Mom.

And so begins the weirdest day of my life.

Because if yesterday was strange, with Lia showing up out of the blue and wrecking my life as I knew it, imagine piling into a convertible with Lia at the helm wearing a scarf and sunglasses like an old movie star. My parents crammed into the backseat, as she looks everywhere but the road and threatens to wreck my life—literally this time. And Dad, who took some convincing to see things my way back when Lia first came to town all those years ago, now giving her tips and advice on how to drive such a big car.

And that's nothing. We come to a halt at the stop sign, Lia giggling away at the wheel, again in her old timey sunglasses and what Mom is calling a "Jackie O scarf." And it just so happens I'm leaning over Lia, trying to show her how to fix the seatbelt when Jen pulls onto our street.

She stops, her window coming down and her mouth open like she might scream. She looks at Lia, me, then back to Mom and Dad with nothing but cold betrayal in her eyes.

"Oh," she says, because what's left to say?

Again, I'm not doing anything wrong, I don't think, and yet, I straighten, run a hand through my hair and tell the truth. "Jen, hey, we're uh, going out for a drive."

"I see," she says, I think. I can hardly hear over the thrumming in my ear, as Jen's glare moves to the backseat where my dad sits, knees pulled up while the look of accomplishment on his face from getting the old car running fades fast. Sort of like the car, which chugs and huffs and hitches like it might conk out. Dad leans forward.

"Give it a little gas, Lia."

Lia basically floors it. The car revs then hitches, and we peel out and away from Jen. Dad sputters, "Oh, um…" while Lia fights the steering wheel, whipping it right as a passing car honks. Mom screams as we fishtail, nearly taking out a mailbox before Lia rights things and lets out a whoop.

"Lia."

"Yeah?" she yells over the wind. "Sorry, that was a lot, huh Kenneth?"

Eventually, we get the car turned around and head back down our street. I wave Jen down as she's driving back the other way. She turns around, and I'm both relieved and disappointed at the same time as she follows us down to Mr. Higgins' place, where the awkwardness grows like a cornfield.

I get out first. Jen, in her Umbro's and t-shirt, looks flushed, and I can't tell if it's from the running or she's mad at me or both. I look back to the car, where Dad flips the seat up and he and Mom scramble out.

"Sorry, we got this old car running. Obviously, Lia doesn't know how to drive."

Dad runs a hand through his hair, smiling as he studies the car. Mom and Lia walk over to us, and Lia has at least removed the sunglasses and scarf, but she's all pumped up from our near death experience.

"Oh my gosh. I'm so sorry. I just gave it a little gas but, well, *kaboom*." She makes an explosion gesture with her hands. "This baby roars."

Jen ignores me completely. She closes her eyes, takes a deep breath, and starts toward Lia with a much too big smile on her face. "Hi, you must be Lia. I'm Jen, Matt's girlfriend. I've heard a lot about you."

"Oh?" Lia looks at me.

Jen's mouth goes tight, but she powers through and tilts her head. "Well, I was stopping by to see if you guys needed any help."

Lia smiles. "Aw, that's so sweet. I haven't gotten much done, there's so much history in there and it's kind of hard to part with anything, if you know what I mean."

"Yeah. You and George Higgins were close, I hear?"

"We were." Lia gazes toward the woods where we've worked to reclaim the path. "Did Matthew tell you how Higgins baptized me in his pond right down there? Didn't he, Matthew."

Jen shakes her head. "Nope, he didn't tell me that. But I knew you two have…had a lot of memories here."

Mom steps in. "Hi, Jen it's good to see you. Ken and I are going to head back."

Mom basically drags Dad away from the car. They start off, Dad glancing back at the Chrysler.

Lia gives him an enthusiastic wave. "Thanks again, Kenneth."

"Sure, no problem. But we still need to flush the radiator and—" Mom jerks him along. "Yeah okay, later then."

Once my parents are gone, Lia announces she needs to "hop to it" because there's all sorts of fabulous clothes in the closet. "Like this scarf," she says with a twirl.

Jen, still with a deranged smile, says we'll be right in. As soon as Lia skips off, the smile slides from her face. "I cannot believe this is happening."

"What? What's happening?"

She shakes her head. "I'm not doing this, Matt. Or should I say, *Matthew*. It's like you're under a spell. Or have you been in love with her this whole time?"

"I'm not in love with her. What, I can't help an old friend?"

She closes her eyes and exhales. "I'm leaving. Pick, right now. Go with me or stay. But I'm not doing both."

"What?" My chest tightens, I glance back to the house. "I don't understand. What are you asking me to do?"

"It's not a difficult question, Matt."

"It's not a fair question, either."

She shrugs. Her eyes are glossy. From the house, the big band sounds drift out to the lawn. "So cute, you gave her that necklace you've been wearing all this time. Don't think I didn't notice."

"It was hers," I say, only then realizing what I've confessed.

Jen closes her eyes and takes a breath. "My point exactly." She turns away, brushing me off. "You know, I just can't..."

"Can't what?"

She glares at me then shakes her head, and I watch, feet planted in the driveway, as she opens the door and gets in her car.

The old Chrysler stares me down, its slanted headlights like a furrowed brow. Jen and I haven't been together that long, but I never thought it would end this way. I never thought a lot of things.

Jen gets turned around, but then she stops the car. And while things I never thought would happen continue, Jen, with shiny bright spite in her eyes, looks back. "Oh, and don't bother coming to the store anymore. I'll have my grandfather mail your last check."

I don't say a word as she tears out of the driveway. And while I feel terrible, I do, I'm just not feeling terrible enough to stop her.

Chapter 9

Lia taps into her "utility fund," and we spend most of the week shuffling furniture in and out of the living room so she can paint the walls a shade of "blue dolphin" she found at Lowes. She paints the brick fireplace a sort of creamy white, and things get brighter as we tear up the carpet and find hardwood floors. She goes minimalist, as she calls it, as we move the couch back in but lose the end tables and all the "grandpa chairs." She refuses to part with the record player.

I never make it to Farmer's to talk to Mr. Yearly, not after receiving what I assume is my final check in the mail for ninety-seven bucks, bringing my total cash flow to three hundred and ten dollars. It sucks, because I liked the job and thought I was pretty good at it. Either way, I'm clearly going to need some work, and fast. In the meantime, Lia keeps me busy with chores and never asks a thing about what happened with Jen or at my job.

She doesn't have a Virginia driver's license so she can't register the car. She throws her shoulders up and down when I ask about a birth certificate, and so I spend a whole afternoon on the phone with someone in Georgia trying to sort it out before we go grocery shopping. She talks about planting a garden, regardless of it being fall. All the time I'm thinking about school and what's going to happen with that situation.

On Thursday I arrive for our first official football practice. News has already spread about Jen and me. Austin, our quarterback, has sent a few texts asking about what happened. Which means, of course, everyone's already heard about Lia as well.

Coach goes over expectations and tries to fire us up with a speech he must have spent the entire summer writing. Other than that it's usual first practice stuff. Expectations. Focus. What he wants from us, what we're capable of, what we... "Hey Matt, you want to join us?"

Amidst some scattered laughter I blink out of my thoughts—about what Lia might be doing right now. What sort of crazy game she's come up with. I shake it off. "Yes, sir."

"Okay, good to know, Crosby. Now give me a lap."

Aiden slaps my head as I get to my feet. The snickering continues. Thing is, I'm not in the mood for practice. After the first lap, I run another, then a third. Coach Wills thinks I'm a go-getter. I'm not, the running helps clear my head.

I get home and shower. I've got one foot out the door when Mom calls after me. "Everything okay?"

"Huh? Oh, yeah."

Mom gives me her best mom smile. She looks like she wants to say more, but so far she and Dad have mostly stayed out of things—haven't said a word about me going down to Lia's every day. Of course, Dad has asked about the car a few times, but that's about it.

With the living room done, Lia's tackled the kitchen, or at least the walls. She's left the hideous yellow floors and cabinets she's labeled mud daisy. As I walk in she sets down her paintbrush and turns to face me.

"So, guess what I did today?"

I try my best not to notice her thin t-shirt covered in paint spatter. But then there's a smudge on her nose and more in her hair. I laugh. "Hmm, finger painted?"

"Haha." She gets to her feet, rocks back, and takes in the walls. She pokes my arm. "I registered for school. You're looking at a fellow senior at Maycomb High."

"Oh."

"Oh?" She jerks her head back. "That's all I get? *Oh*. Because if I remember correctly you were all against me dropping out. I thought you would be thrilled."

Of all the distractions in my life, this one promises to do me in. I shake it off. "No, I am."

Lia at Maycomb. I take a breath. I remember wondering this same thing as an incoming freshman. What in the world would Lia be like at school? But she left before I ever found out. Now it's happening all over again.

"You're not happy." She sighs and turns back to her walls. "I promise I won't interfere with your social life. But I need to finish school. And then, maybe even college." She shoots me a look. "You know, I was really expecting a different reaction."

"Lia, that's awesome, I'm just, surprised."

She smiles. "I will walk around like this." She stares at her feet. "Pretending not to know you. I won't embarrass you, okay?"

"What? No. Lia that's awesome, really. I'm happy, okay? It was a tough practice."

"Oh, that's right, football." Then, lighting up again. "Guess what I found."

I smile, despite everything. "Another car?"

"Ha, no. Come on."

She lunges for the kitchen table where notes and scraps of paper, ledgers, books, and receipts lay scattered across the surface. A map of the property. She looks at me, then to the table. I can't stop staring at the paint on her nose.

"Ready for some treasure hunting?"

I laugh. She thrusts a paper at me. It's Mr. Higgins' will and final testament.

She points, her nail chipped and spotted with paint, under Article IV, where it states what he's leaving to Lia. She leans in close, her hair tickling my nose as she taps where it's all "hereby" this and that and Lia's name and finally—

What is found on this land shall go to the owner, Lia Banks, and...

I look up. "How is this a clue?"

She rips the page away from me with a sigh. "What is *found* on this *land*? Sort of odd language, don't you think?"

"Um, sure?"

Lia turns away from me. "Useless, Matthew. Okay, Mr. *Sure*. Why don't you have a look at this."

She shuffles through some papers, then thrusts a wrinkled, paint splattered, handwritten note at me. She takes a step back and stands with her arms crossed, head cocked, and nods for me to read.

The compartments of our lives hold the key to what we're seeking. Wear the gloves that fit you well. -GH

"He wrote this?"

Lia nods.

"Where was it?"

Both eyebrows go up. "In the drawer with the registration and keys."

"Why didn't you tell me about it?"

She throws her hands out. "Because I knew you would make fun of me!"

"No, I wouldn't." I read it again, then look to her. "But what, I don't..."

She rolls her eyes. "Okay, I'll bring you up to speed. While you were bashing your head in on the football field, I was solving mysteries. The car. The glove compartment."

"Oh, okay."

"Yeah, oh. Now, ready for the rest? Here's what I found in the glove compartment."

"Couldn't you have just led with that?"

She blows a strand of hair from her face and gives me the next note.

And where the pines stand, and the buzzards roost, the golden sun shall set and lead the way.

And it's here, or near, or down below, where the rock and the tree grow together.

"Some kind of poem."

She wipes back her hair, and for a second I'm lost in every tangle and curl, every natural highlight, until she blinks with a smile. "What?"

"Huh? Oh, nothing." I set my eyes back to the crumpled page. "Just, could be a clue, or it could be a poem. Where did you find this?"

She flashes another smile. "It could be both. Remember there was a note that got me to the car, or have you conveniently forgotten that tidbit?"

And to think I'd forgotten how dramatic she is about everything. How everything she says is like an old sitcom or movie. But this poem, the wording, maybe she's onto something. "Huh? Well, that's weird."

"I don't think it's so weird, Matthew. I think it's a treasure hunt."

Who talks this way? Again, I tell myself she's going to Maycomb High. Lia, the most fascinating person I've ever known, who's morphed into this beautiful woman with full lips and smooth skin yet still holds me captive with her magical eyes, is going to my high school.

I turn back to her. "Well, okay. What now?"

She squeals, picks up my hands, and smiles. "Now, we hunt!"

Chapter 10

We hit the grove of pine trees armed with a shovel and a crumpled poem. The turkey buzzards keep an eye on us while squabbling for room on the limbs. Lia keeps looking up, sort of ducking her head, afraid of what might drop.

Preacher Higgins fought the birds vigilantly, trying all sorts of different tactics to get them to leave. He used to play his trusty bugle to scare them away. But they've never left, and now, as they watch us, I wonder what they've seen. But that reminds me. "Hey, have you seen an old bugle in the house?"

Lia turns to me with a smile. "A what?"

I explain it to her. She laughs, says she hasn't seen it, then gets back to an episode of Treasure Seekers she watched in a tiny hotel room in Oregon when it wouldn't stop raining.

I turn away from the buzzards. "When were you in Oregon?"

Lia shrugs. She toes something buried beneath the pine needles. "Oh, last summer. I sort of happened upon the west coast."

"How does one just happen upon the other side of the country?"

She plows in with the shovel. "Well, I was working a camp out in Northern California. And then I joined this sketch comedy troupe. It was fun, but I started seeing this guy, who turned out to be a major jerk."

A major stab of jealousy finds my chest, even as I know it's ridiculous. In three years what did I expect, her to join the convent? I laugh to cover it up, then for some reason I say, "Have you had a lot of boyfriends?"

She pops her head up from the digging. "Hey, what kind of question is that?"

"I, no…I don't know, just talking I guess." I turn away because my face is on fire.

She laughs. "No, I have not. I refuse to make the same mistakes as my mother."

"Oh," I manage, happy to put it behind us.

She stretches. "But Williford was a mistake. A big time mistake."

I stop, wondering if she's going to continue. She kneels, pokes at something under the pine needles, then stands. "He was part of the crew, not the troupe but the production. He was shy and quiet but with this cute little smile. He took me out to the movies, on a date. It was so old fashioned."

"Oh, okay." I pretend to be really interested in a rock near the clearing where the barbeque pit is, or used to be, but is all overgrown now. I'm really not wanting to hear about Lia's love life, which she now has no problem going on about.

"Well, at first I thought it was sweet. But then, I don't know, he just sort of changed. He became super jealous, clingy, like he owned me. We'd been on like three dates and he was acting like we were married. And then one night, well, he kissed me and I didn't want to be kissed. And he…" she shakes off the memory. "Anyway, Willie was not who I thought he was, so I left him a note, and probably a limp, got in my car and drove to Oregon. Where I watched Treasure Hunters." She shrugs. "You know."

"So, you did sketch comedy?"

She turns to me, arching her brow. "I'm quite hysterical, Matthew."

"That's cool. Really cool."

"Yeah, the Pinwheels. I went to one of the shows, they brought me on stage, and it was so much fun. After the show they offered me a spot." She shrugs. "We traveled all over the place. Small shows, mostly, but they were always packed, lots of improv. What, why are you looking at me like that?"

I shake my head, getting over my jealousy, getting over myself. "What have you *not* done?"

"I have not found this treasure, for one."

We take a seat on the old rock wall. The barbeque is covered in pine needles and leaves, but it's still one of my favorite places, how it's hidden but still overlooks the woods. Lia, sitting close so our legs touch, smells like vanilla, dirt and sweat, shampoo all at once.

She turns to me, her eyes roaming the backdrop. "Isn't this beautiful?"

I nod.

"Hey, you okay?"

I look off, to the woods. "I never thought I'd see you again, Lia."

Her gaze falls to her running shoes. She knocks them together. "Yeah, I know. Mr. Higgins said you'd moved on, that you were doing well for yourself."

"I had no idea you two were in touch. I wish he would have told me."

She stares off, and it feels like I'm making things weird. Until she hops up and spins around. "Well, I'm really glad I came back."

"Did you ever think about selling the house, just taking the money?"

She bites her lip. "Well yeah, of course. But...I could never do that. Mr. Higgins helped me so much."

"Yeah, how?"

"Well, pep talks and stuff. He said I had to trust God. I had to keep the faith and stay positive. Not easy to do when your mom's looking at five to seven, you know?"

"Oh wow. Lia, I'm really sorry."

A quick shrug of the shoulders. "It's her own fault."

"Still."

"Thanks."

"Yeah. So this treasure, did he ever mention it before, when you guys would talk?"

She sets the shovel on her shoulder. "You know, I'm trying to remember. We weren't besties or anything. We didn't talk often, just here and there."

"More than us."

She sets the shovel down. Her shoulders drop, and she starts to say something but doesn't. My heart lunges as she takes a step closer to me. Birds squawk over our heads, bugs are chirring. Lia's eyes don't leave mine. She takes one of my hands. "I thought about you all the time."

"Yeah." I laugh, look away. "I dreamed about you."

Lia closes her eyes and moves closer, inches from my face. "I hope they weren't bad dreams." She smiles, just a bit, as her gaze falls to my lips. Her hair tickles my arm. I take a breath then I'm leaning closer, when two blasts of a horn make us jump.

Lia shrieks. Through the trees I can spot a white truck, purple and orange letters. Fed Ex barreling down the driveway.

We look at each other. Lia lets out a "Oh?" then takes off running. "Look, it's the present truck!"

I catch up to her in the driveway. The driver shimmies his way out of the truck as we rush up to him. He looks at the tablet in his hand. "Lia Banks?"

Lia nods, practically jumping in place. He checks the tablet again. "Delivery for you."

"What is it?" Lia asks, like a little girl on Christmas morning.

The man makes his way for the back, grumbling, "A delivery."

With his back to her, Lia sticks her tongue out at him. He fiddles with the latch at the back. Lia wiggles her eyebrows at me.

"Here it is." He consults his tablet once again. "Sterling Fields, Attorney at Law. Sounds fancy."

Lia claps. "Yes. It's here!"

I look at her, the guy stares. "What's here?"

Lia signs the digital screen, and the guy hands us a box like a laptop might come in. "You kids have fun."

And then he's putting the truck in gear.

"Well," Lia says, holding up the package. "Come on."

"Can you tell me what's going on?"

"Well, since you're so impatient, *Sterling*," she says with flourish, "contacted me a few weeks back. Turns out, Mr. Higgins' paintings were on display at a gallery in Richmond. Did you know that? Bet you didn't."

I shake my head. *Paintings?*

"Right, you didn't. Because you never came down here." She shoots me a pout. "Anyway, Sterling asked if I wanted to sell them, apparently they'd "fetch a good price," to quote Kenneth. He sent a galley down, and I was looking through them, and they're all really, really good, obviously. One of Jolene, another of the mountains. But then I thought about it, how it would be best if they stay on display for people to enjoy. So I bequeathed them to the museum. All but one." She taps the box.

I laugh. "Did you just say *bequeathed?*"

She smacks my arm. I nod at the package. "Okay, but what is this one?"

She holds it up, her lips curving into a smile. "*This* one." She leans into me, her eyes wide. "This one I had to have. It's going over the fireplace."

Inside, Lia shows me the prints of Higgins' work. And she's right, he was good. Who knew? I'm still staring at the portrait of Jolene when Lia grabs a knife and carefully drags it down the edge of the box. She unfolds sides and removes the packing and then she cocks her head, her lips sort of jutting out.

"What?"

She closes her eyes and turns the painting to me.

"Oh," I say, and hardly manage that much.

It's a painting of a boy and a girl holding hands on the dock. The water is still, a few rings that almost look like they're growing. A canoe lays abandoned in the tall grass at the edge. The setting sun burns orange and yellow around them, filtering through the trees. The girl has wild hair with natural highlights.

The boy only stares into her eyes.

Chapter 11

After Lia basically disappeared right before school started freshman year, I was devastated. I stayed in my room, wondering, dreaming, wishing, until at some point I came out and began going through the motions of becoming a freshman at Maycomb High.

I entered high school forever changed by Lia. But then, as the weeks went by, as the grind that was high school took hold, a bit of the shine slipped off the memories. At the end of the year I had surgery on my chest to fix the dip that had haunted me for years, the dip Lia said wasn't so bad. I healed. I still thought about Lia, still wore the dog tag, but I also thought about new friends, new girls, new experiences.

During sophomore year, I was working with Dad and my body was changing. I gained inches and muscles and suddenly things weren't looking so awful for me. And the jobs with Dad usually left me doing the heavy lifting. Then one day he looked at me and smiled. We were the same height.

The football coach came calling in eleventh grade, and Dad was grinning and Mom was a little worried, but everyone thought I should do it. More new friends, more girls. I hit the field and it all came easy.

And still I dreamed about Lia.

She'd taught me so much. How to be confident. To be brave enough to face my fears. But mostly she taught me how to be myself.

Maybe that's why I never took the dog tag off, or never quit dreaming about her at night. Maybe I knew, or hoped, that wherever she was she felt it too—what I held in my heart.

Now here she is, back in Maycomb, on my street. And I don't know what to do.

It's the weekend before school starts, and Lia and I have made zero new discoveries with the whole Treasure hunt. On Friday evening, after another long, hot practice, I drag myself down to Higgins' place when it occurs to me that maybe the old preacher is orchestrating all of this from the grave.

Lia living in his house, the painting, the poetic clues—all of it seems too coincidental. But it's crazy to think it was his plan to bring us back together, even if that seems like it's exactly what he is doing.

And the other day, when we almost kissed, or at least I think we almost kissed, leaves me buzzing with anticipation, wondering what might happen next. It also leaves me feeling guiltier than ever.

Jen hasn't called or texted, and I hate to think of how weird it's going to be on Monday. But once I spot Lia, in the car with the top down, waiting for me, well, all is forgotten.

I tell her she can't drive because she doesn't have a license, not to mention the license plates are from 2005. She rolls her eyes and slides to the passenger side.

"Fine, you drive. It's insured."

I hop in, gripping the huge, round steering wheel. "Well, we're only going up the street, I guess."

"I guess," she mocks me in a deep voice.

You'd think Lia was in a parade by way she waves to people in passing as she directs me to pull in at Dairy Queen, where she leans over me to place her order. I pretend it's no big deal, the touch of her arms, the heat of her breath as she giggles and says how it's all so 1950's. Big deal or not, I must be feeling guilty as I look around, just waiting to see who sees us. It doesn't take long.

After we place our order, we pull off to a space to wait. I nudge Lia. "Remember Ethan?"

She flops back down to her seat and turns to me, her hair in her face, before she gazes past me and her eyes widen. "Oh my gosh."

Ethan Moore was a childhood friend, sort of. We played baseball, only I was awful, and he had no problems letting me know it. He nicknamed me Bowl. He also teased me about Lia—about her hair and her eyes and her darker skin—before he turned around and asked her out.

Again, Lia leans over me to get a better look at him. "He's so short. Did he shrink?"

I stifle a laugh. Ethan was always the tallest, strongest, and biggest kid around, but it turned out he'd done all his growing before most of us started. Now, as I'm six three, I tower over him, and it's strange to think how he used to seem so big.

I try to get Lia under control but it's too late. Ethan stops when he sees us, smiles, and struts over. He fixes his baseball cap, which he's never without. He still plays baseball, and he's a decent shortstop for Maycomb. Compact and quick. Just, really short.

He starts over with a head nod. "Yo, Matty, what is up?"

Somewhere along the line, Ethan decided he was going to be the most gangster baseball player in Maycomb. And he has succeeded. I watch as his gaze leaves me and finds Lia, and his eyes widen with surprise. It takes him a second, when Lia shakes her hair from her face, licks her lips and says, "Hi, Ethan."

He looks at me, then back to her, his cocky smile finding its stride. "Oh damn. Lia, is that you?"

"Uh huh." She smiles and I can feel her giggling against me. I nudge her to stop, but she's having too much fun.

"Oh. What in the f—" he looks left and right again, cups his hands to his mouth. "Yo, this is crazy."

Lia smiles. "Isn't it?"

"Damn, you look fine."

Lia opens her mouth, shuts it, blinks a few times then tries again. "Well thank you Ethan, you look..." she shrugs, but Ethan doesn't take offense because he's too busy grinning and nodding at me. If I thought this would be weird, I was wrong. It's torture.

"Well, we're going to, uh…" I look back toward the guy bringing out our order.

"Ah, okay, I got you," he says, as though I'd suggested something lurid.

Before I can blink, Lia leaps out of the car without opening the door. She meets the guy with our order and grabs the ice cream cones. Ethan's head swivels to better stare.

I still can't believe I spent middle school looking up to that guy—both figuratively and literally. He's talking baseball as I tell him we have to go. Lia returns to my side of the car where she smiles at him again, and he starts off, nearly tripping as he walks away. I shake my head. "I think we should take our ice cream to go."

Lia rolls her eyes playfully as she leans against the car, licks her ice cream cone, and glances down to me. "Still ashamed of me, huh?"

I start to speak but I can't. I have no words. Lia walks around to the other side and leaps into the car.

When we get back, she wants to work on the path down to the pond. Before I can ask, we're tromping through the woods, cutting through the undergrowth, ducking tree limbs, and getting caught in the briars. We get the path mostly cleared, although I'm going to need the chainsaw for the fallen pine tree.

At the pond she stops, hands on her hips, tilting her head left then right. "It's like we never left."

Before I can argue with her, she takes off for the old canoe. I call out. "Do I have to remind you about snakes?"

She turns to me. "You do not, but if we do encounter snakes, I have no doubt you will ditch me without a second's thought and go running away screaming like a girl."

I sigh. One time we took the canoe out, and it wasn't until we were out on the water that I discovered a snake at our feet. I may have bailed without warning. "Ah, you remember that?"

"How could I forget?"

She has me drag the canoe out, but it's busted in two places. Lia stares at it in disbelief.

"I might be able to fix it."

She nods, wipes her hands clean. "I'm sure you can."

We stand next to each other, watching the sun sink into the horizon, almost like the painting. But this is no painting, this is real. It might feel like we're hidden away in these woods—like we're strokes of a paint brush—but we're not hidden at all. And I'm not too sure where Jen and I stand after the other day, but if we're still together, I'm not being the best boyfriend right now.

A week and a half ago I knew exactly what to expect. I had it all mapped out and felt like I was in control of my future. Now we have a new map, written in riddles by a preacher playing one last prank on us.

Lia grabs my hand and we take a seat on the dock. Maybe we can hide for just a little bit longer.

Chapter 12

When we get back to the house the lightning bugs are out. I'm covered in welts and bites, and Lia's picking pieces of sticks and twigs from her hair.

"Well, that was a bust," she says as we get back inside. She puts a record on, some sort of old jazzy singing that would be ridiculous if anyone else in the world played it.

I stand in the room, wondering whether to sit and stay or get home. While my Dad's come a long way, he has made it clear I am not to be in the house at night, or alone, or at all, really.

"Oh," she lights up suddenly. "Want to see my class schedule?"

"Yeah, sure. "

"I think they put me in all remedial classes. They really had no idea what to do with me just showing up like that."

That makes two of us, I'm thinking as she plops down on the couch. "So did you, like, were you in school last year?"

She smiles, shrugs. "Sort of. Most of my education has been on the fly, sort of like one big field trip. Learn by doing, you know?"

"I guess." I check her schedule, and yep, she's got the most basic of classes. English Lit. Sociology. They put her in Geometry, and she's even got P.E., something I haven't taken since tenth grade.

"Hey, you're in Musical Theatre?"

She blows out her cheeks.

I set the schedule on my lap. "Lia, I've heard you sing."

She coughs, blinks, and then she can't hold it anymore. "I know, right? Joke's on them!"

"Wow, that's going to be interesting. And Spanish II? That a joke too?"

She sets a hand to her chest. *"Creo que lo hare' bien."*

I look to the ceiling. "Of course you speak Spanish."

"Sí." She shrugs. "A little."

"Let me guess, you lived in Mexico?"

"No, dork. I've watched a lot of Latin soap operas."

She smiles and I notice she still has that little chip in her front tooth and I'm staring at her, thinking, *don't try to kiss her, don't try to kiss her* when my phone buzzes and I jump.

I don't reach for the phone, but Lia smiles. "I think you should call Jen and explain."

"Explain what?"

Lia gets to her feet and starts for the kitchen, talking over her shoulder. "That we're old friends. She's your girlfriend after all, and I feel like I've messed things up for you."

Ouch. So the pond just now, holding my hand, or the other day, under the pine trees, it didn't mean much. I get up and follow her to the kitchen. "Well, she did get me fired. And honestly we weren't that close. We never talked about much—school, sports, friends." I force myself to stop pleading my case to Lia.

She pours a glass of water, turns around and takes a sip, leaning against the sink. She lowers the glass and stares at me. It knocks me back.

I swallow down the sudden lump in my throat. "What?"

She smiles. "Nothing. You're just, so different. But the same."

I look around. "Yeah, you too."

She squints at me. "How am I different?"

I shoot her a look. "Lia, come on."

She only stares at me, her eyes pinning me down. I can't tell what's happening. "Come on, what?"

The clock ticks off five seconds, ten. I roll my eyes and do my best Ethan impression. "Damn girl, you're fine."

She finally breaks with a smile. "And you're not bad yourself." Then she turns back to the sink, and I'm left wondering. My phone buzzes again.

"You should probably get that," she sings.

I step outside and find the message is from Jen.

So it was that easy? I can't believe you.

I call her. She's crying.

"Jen."

"What?" she hisses.

"Jen, what's going on?"

"Shouldn't I ask you that?"

"Well, I lost my job." I cringe as the words come out of my mouth. What a dumb thing to say.

"That's what you're worried about? You're out on dates for everyone to see, and you're calling me back about your job?"

"No, I just mean, I..." I look back to Lia's house.

"I need to talk to you, okay? In person. You owe me that much, at least."

"Okay."

I agree to come to her house. But when I walk back in to tell Lia I'm leaving I find her on the floor, cross legged, already in a box, reading through old sermons and books.

She looks up and smiles. "I'm looking for more clues."

"Oh." I sort of laugh, wanting nothing more in the world than to take a seat on the floor with her and pick through Higgins' old things, listen to whatever craziness falls out of her mouth. But I can't do that to Jen. She's right, I owe her that much. I hook a thumb toward the door. "So, um. I have to go, but I can be down tomorrow?"

She nods. "You don't have to, Matthew. It's okay."

"No, I want to, really. But I have to go take care of something."

She doesn't turn around. "Yep."

I linger at the door. The lamp casting a cozy glow, the old timey horns and music on the record player. She looks back at me again and smiles. I walk over and sit. Our knees touch.

"I've got a few minutes, I guess."

JEN LIVES in the newer part of Maycomb. A nice subdivision with clean curbs and large lots. Dad said it's where they used to ride dirt bikes as a kid. He likes to drive through the new neighborhoods, taking in the lush grass and pruned trees, gazing off at something only he can see. *Here, we'd race around that corner, right here, oh and we had a jump there and...*

Mrs. Yearly greets me with a solemn smile. "Matt, please come in."

It's quiet in the Yearly's house. Too quiet. Walking inside, it's clear I'm the villain in this scene. It probably doesn't help that I'm late, that I almost turned around five times on the short drive over.

Mrs. Yearly escorts me to the den, where I've been a hundred times. Jen sits slumped on the couch watching TV. Her face is flushed red and a box of tissues sits on the coffee table. My stomach drops. This is not where I want to be.

Mrs. Yearly leaves us alone. Jen doesn't say a word as I enter and find a seat a cushion away. She only stares at the TV screen where some reality show has entered the super dramatic judging stage.

"Hey," I say softly. She sniffles and I plod ahead. "Look, I'm sorry about...everything."

I can't say what *everything* is, it feels like I'm throwing a blanket over the whole situation, which is probably why Jen glares at me, her eyes puffy and red. "Like what, cheating on me?"

"What?" I scoot to the edge of the sofa, glance to the doorway. Is that what she told her mom? No wonder I got the silent treatment. "Jen, I didn't—hey, I'm not cheating on you."

I don't sound confident. And my ankles are covered in dirt from the pond, my shirt with hitchhikers from the woods. I can't stop thinking about the other day under the pine trees, what might have happened had the Fed Ex guy not shown up. Or whatever almost happened in the kitchen when my phone buzzed. But still, technically I haven't *cheated*. Right?

Jen turns to me with a harsh stare. "Come on, Matt. Please, at least treat me with some respect. Even if you haven't, you..."

Then she's crying again. New tears, and maybe she's right, I have cheated on her, not physically, but still. Now I feel trapped in this room, this house, this subdivision where my dad used to ride dirt bikes.

"Jen."

"I just, I thought we'd start this year and go to homecoming and prom and those things. And now it's..."

"We will." Again, it isn't convincing, but it's enough.

She stops and looks up at me with wet eyes. "Really?"

I'm surprised at the sudden change in her voice. The hopefulness. I take a breath and try to make myself believe it. "Yeah, of course."

I'm a terrible person. A terrible, terrible human being. I'm only saying what she wants to hear. But I can't take it, I can't stay in this dark room in this quiet house and have her whimpering like this. Even as my dad would tell me to do the right thing, the right thing isn't always so easy.

She launches into me with a hug. "Oh, Matt, I'm so glad. I was so worried..."

I hug her back awkwardly, wondering what in the world I've just done.

Chapter 13

The first day of school arrives. I'm up by seven and dressed and ready to go fifteen minutes later. Jen wanted to pick me up for some big first day of school breakfast, but I came up with an excuse about helping Mom. I wasn't quite ready for a mental war with Sarah and Courtney.

In the kitchen, Mom kisses me on the cheek. "I just can't believe it."

"Mom, don't start."

"What, it's, you're a senior in high school, Matt. Where did the time go?"

She's being extra corny, but there is some truth to what she's saying. Senior year has come and this was supposed to be easy street. But nothing is easy now. Not even close.

I didn't see Lia Saturday or Sunday. I didn't run down there when it was all I thought about. I watched movies with Jen yesterday, and with each boom of thunder I wondered if Lia still liked to count off the seconds between the flashes in the sky and the rumbles in the clouds.

And so now here I am, pulling into Maycomb High School. A liar. A fraud. A horrible person. I set Mom's car in park and take in the lot. James and Austin, a couple of teammates, are leaning against Austin's shiny black truck, laughing and having a good time. They see me and nod. I nod back, take a breath, and tell myself I might as well get moving.

I get out of the car, looking around, thinking of all the days I counted off until it was finally my turn. The sky is a vivid blue, the sun already warm, and it's everything I could want for the first day of senior year. I start for Austin and James when I hear the roar of a 1962 Chrysler Newport pulling in.

The top is down, because of course it is. Lia's hair's a nest of wild as she slings the car dangerously around where it comes to a halt right beside me. She gathers what looks like a burlap sack, and like a gymnast, she slings herself over the door.

I laugh. "Those things open, you know."

She turns and looks at the car. Her sky blue shirt is unbuttoned midway, revealing a tank top. The sleeves rolled up. Khaki shorts. Judging by Austin and James' and every other guy's reaction, she's pulling it off.

She throws her hand on my chest for balance as she fixes her shoe. "Wow, so have you ever seen Teen Wolf?"

I forget whatever I was about to say and nod that I have. She shakes her head wildly. "No, not the stupid show, the old movie."

I must still look confused because she laughs. "You know," she lowers her voice. "'Give me, a keg, of beer.' That one?"

We've basically got an audience now. I scratch my head. "What?"

She ignores me. "The movie, it's exactly like this." She surveys the lot. "There. You've got the stoners, preps, loners…" She cocks a brow at me. "The jocks." She gets the shoe fixed and arches her back. "All that's missing is the lettermen jackets."

She's still pointing out different cliques when Jen's car pulls into the lot. And who is sitting beside her? Only my favorite Porter Grill waitress, Courtney.

They don't hide their staring. Jen's mouth is tight and her window is up, but I can guess what she's saying. And Austin and the guys are watching, too.

Lia is back to quoting movies when three girls climb out of Jen's car and come straight for us. Jen scoots up beside me and takes my hand. She looks at Lia. "Hi, Lia."

Lia turns and smiles. "Hi, Jen. Happy first day of school."

Courtney does some sort of *pfft* thing with her mouth. I rock back on my heels, onstage for the entire parking lot as Jen, through a clenched smile, says, "I didn't know you were going to Maycomb this year. What a surprise."

Lia bobs her head. "Yeah, I was going to get my GED, but I figured, you know what? Let's give this thing a shot."

I laugh way too hard. "She's kidding. Lia's going to go to vet school. Right, Lia?"

Now the girls are laughing and everything is wrong. It's like I'd said astronaut. Lia turns to me, her eyes giving away nothing. "Well, I guess I'll go look for my class. Bye."

Before I can offer to help, Lia smiles and walks toward the school. Courtney and Sarah exchange smirks. "Wow."

By the time I get to first period I'm in a trance. Everything is off, wrong, nothing feels right. Austin takes the desk next to me. "Hey, man, that's awesome about Jen, right?"

"Huh? What is?"

Austin raises an eyebrow, shoots me a smirk. "Dude, you're kidding, right? She was named preseason all-district." He looks at me closer. "Please tell me you're kidding."

"That's awesome. "I'll..."

He shakes his head. "Oh, man. Come on, Matty."

Later that morning I spot Lia in the halls. She's at her locker, and I want to ask her about Musical Theatre, but she's already chatting up a group of guys—theater types. Maybe she didn't bomb after all. She sees me and lights up with a wave. I wave back and then she's gone.

Jen finds me at lunch. I'm about to congratulate her but something's on her mind. "Oh. My. Gosh." The way she's gushing could only mean Lia.

"What?"

"Your little friend, she's making waves."

"Yeah, how?"

"She's trying out for the lead in *Garden Variety*."

"Is that the fall play?" I smile. "Really? That's awesome."

Jen looks at me like I've lost my mind. "Um, okay. Sarah's been in drama for three years, and now this crazy chick thinks she's going to waltz in and land the lead role?"

"Well, that's why they have auditions, right?"

"Okay just, never mind." Jen looks away.

I pretend I'm not looking for Lia in the cafeteria. "Oh, hey, congrats on All District. Although, not much of a surprise, right?"

Jen smiles, her irritation melting some. "Oh, thanks," she says, no big deal and all.

"No really," I say, trying my best to scrounge up some enthusiasm. When did I become so awful? Why am I faking it so hard? "I think it's great."

"Thanks, Matt," she says. "Well, I gotta go." She gives me a quick hug and then she's off.

News of Lia spreads fast, and by the time I catch a glimpse of her she's in the gym, leading a yoga session with some underclassmen.

I stop and she sees me and pops up. "Matthew, hi."

She runs out to me, slightly out of breath. "Oh my gosh I love gym!"

I look over her shoulder. "Jim? Where is he? Point him out."

She gushes, slaps me on the chest. "Seriously, can I just take gym all day? I'm starting a yoga club."

I shake my head, laughing. Not even one day in and Lia has made quite the mark. "You're not even dressed out."

She looks down, still in her khaki shorts, but she's shed the button down for the tank. "I know, I've got to get the hang of this high school thing, right?"

Behind her, a group of boys gather, all too eager to sign up for yoga. I look at Lia and resist the urge to ask her if we can hop in the Chrysler and leave.

"Looks like you're doing just fine."

Chapter 14

Jen calls after practice. She's at Crave Sub, and Austin and some of the football guys are already there. It's loud, and Jen keeps laughing at something Austin says, and maybe I should be jealous but I'm not. I tell her I'm tired and that I've got some things to do at home, even as I'm walking out the door and down the street.

I'm nearly at Higgins' driveway when we hang up and I hear the yelps. Then laughter. I peek around the bushes and find Lia chasing a goat. I stop, the phone at my side, watching her run around in circles until she sees me and throws her hands up.

"Don't just stand there, Matthew! I need some help!"

"Okay, this is happening," I say to myself, and join the goat chase.

The goat, shiny black with a white chin, is surprisingly fast and does not want to be caught. He weaves around a tree, stops, juts his head out with his little horns, then runs off again. Lia screams at me for giving up so easily, but it's hard to run when you're laughing so hard.

I motion for Lia to go the other way while I sort of herd the goat back around the tree. She dives, both arms out, and misses completely as the goat runs for the woods.

I rush over to help Lia to her feet. She dusts off her backside, and I figure it's time for the obvious question. "Why do you have a goat?"

She shoots me a look, catching her breath. "You have to ask?"

Fair enough. We plunge into the woods, chasing this goat who tears through the thorns and everything else without regard. Lia calls after him. "Linus, get back here."

"Linus?" I ask, still trying to make my way through the thickets. "Seriously?"

"Yes, *Linus*." She stares me down until there's a snap of a twig and she turns. "There he is!"

We find him at the pond. He trots around the water and Lia sends me around the back, the more likely to be snake infested route. She approaches Linus with a soft voice, and I stop and watch as the goat kind of falls into her.

"Thattaboy."

I tromp back around, and Lia has her arms around his neck, more hugging than pulling. She introduces me to Linus, the goat she found on Craigslist for free.

I laugh, but I should have known. "What's next? Chickens?"

"Maybe," she says defiantly. She strokes the goat's chin and he seems content. I step forward and scratch his head. He leans into my hand.

Lia beams. "Aww, he likes you."

He sort of butts my hand, and I step back, until I realize he's not angry but showing affection. "Okay, Linus. Welcome to the farm."

We manage to coax Linus up to the yard. I find some fence panels and scrap wood in the back and start on a makeshift pen. It probably won't hold, but it's all we have for now.

I'm drenched with sweat and filthy from the mud stained two-by-fours when I find Lia, and Linus, in the living room.

"He's staying inside?"

Lia cocks her head. "For now." She looks me up and down. "What happened to you?"

"I, nothing."

Lia tells me about the play. I ask her how much experience she has and she looks me over. "A lifetime."

"Well it sounds like you had no trouble fitting in. And the yoga class is a hit, it seems. From what I saw."

I say it as a jab but she turns to me with a smile. "Yes. How cool is that?"

I laugh until she punches my arm. "Why were you being so weird today?"

Why was I being weird? I reach over and scratch Linus's head. He lays his head into me. "Was I? I don't know, I guess it's just weird, with you being there."

"Do you want me to pretend I don't know you?" She's serious.

This gorgeous girl is asking if I want her to pretend I don't know her at school. It would be funny, if I could figure out what was going on between us.

"What? No way. And I'm coming to your audition."

I FIX up the pen some more before Lia declares it's time to go looking for the treasure, which she's still convinced is under the pine trees. I wouldn't call it treasure, but we do find three horseshoes, an old metal rake, some wine bottles, and what Lia swears are Native American arrowheads. They're sort of triangular rocks, but she's so convinced I let her run with it.

It's nearly dark when we stop at the barbeque pit, sweaty and filthy and empty handed. Lia sits back, one leg up. "Okay, so maybe not under the trees. I need to look over the clues again. And check on Linus."

"Oh yeah, your goat, the one in the house."

"Shut up." She hops up and shoves past me, but I grab her hand. We're walking up the path and she's in my face teasing me about chasing Linus and I'm teasing her back about having a pet goat when Jen's car pulls in the driveway.

Lia takes her hand back. I stop in my tracks, wondering what she's doing here as she gets out, looks us over. Her face goes tight, but she recovers with a fake smile. "Oh, hi, Matt I was looking for you. Hi, Lia," she says with a bit of politeness tacked on at the end.

Lia smiles. "Hi." The three of us stand there for a minute when there's a banging sound from the house. "Oh, that's Linus."

Lia sprints off and Jen furrows her brow and says, "Who's Linus?" but I'm already trailing after Lia.

Another bang as we open the door. Lia stops, and I knock into her. She covers her mouth. Linus looks up from the couch, a pillow in his mouth. There's stuffing everywhere. "Uh oh."

"Bad Linus." Lia shoos him off the couch. He's also eaten three or four records, a pair of shoes, and the curtain off the main window.

Jen steps in behind us. "What in the world?"

I help Lia scoot Linus off the couch. Jen let's out a yelp and runs for the car as we herd the goat into the pen.

Lia smiles at me. "I need to housetrain him, that's all."

"Yeah, that's all."

We get Linus settled, where I can't imagine him staying. If he doesn't break out, Lia will invite him back in soon.

I'm tightening up the fence wires in one of the corners when Jen returns. "So, um, Matt?"

It's strange, wrong, hearing Jen's voice at Lia's house. I'm unsure how to act when Lia looks at me then sighs. "Well, I have a lot of cleaning up to do."

"I can help. If you want?"

Jen glares at me. Lia shakes her head. "No, that's okay. Thanks for making the pen." She looks back, where the goat is already gnawing on the pallet. "I think Linus likes it."

I follow Jen out to the car, still confused, looking back because I hate that Lia has to clean up everything by herself.

Jen hops in the car, and I'm tempted to keep walking home. Instead I fall into the passenger seat. The tattered curtain moves in the window, Lia trying to take them down. She sees me and waves.

Jen watches it all, then finally turns the key. "You know, she's not *that* pretty."

I'm shaken from my thoughts. "What?"

Jen starts the car and puts it in gear. "Oh, nothing. It's just that Sarah was saying how the guys were going on about the new girl and how she's so hot. Sure, I guess, but she's not like..." She brushes it off. "Never mind. It doesn't matter."

I know she's trying to get something out of me. I let out a yawn. "Jen, I'm really tired. With practice and..."

"And chasing goats around and all..."

"So were you like, in the neighborhood, or?"

She gets backed out of the driveway, turns around, but stops. The dashboard lights the side of her face. "What's happened to us, Matt?"

Not this again. I know we're close to tear territory, and I'm too exhausted to do all of this right now. "Nothing's happened. An old friend has moved back to town, and I'm just helping her."

Jen nods her head slowly. "And that's all?"

"Yes."

"And that's why you never take your phone with you anymore?"

I pat my pockets. Maybe it fell out during the goat chase. "I honestly don't know where my phone is right now."

"Exactly. Gosh, you're acting so weird now. You're too... When was the last time you called me, Matt? Or held my hand? Or even hugged me?"

I reach for her hand but she takes it back, drops it in her lap. "Can you please try to see this from my perspective? What if some guy I used to know moved to town and suddenly I was at his house all the time—where he lives alone. Would that be okay?"

"I don't know, Jen."

"I don't either."

Eventually she drives up to my house. I get out. Jen leaves with a gust of whatevers. I don't know what she wants. She doesn't seem to like me so much but doesn't want me at Lia's.

In bed that night I stare at the ceiling. The same ceiling I stared at that summer after I'd sneak out with Lia and we'd go on some wild moonlight adventure.

I look at my window. The moon is out.

I wonder what she's doing right now.

Chapter 15

School only gets weirder. Lia and I have no classes together so I hardly see her, yet she's the topic of almost every conversation I find myself around that morning.

Some of my teammates want to know more. A few guys in class talk about the new girl with the convertible. How she's sort of weird—*what's up with her attitude?* —but so hot. It's all I can do not to roll my eyes. Ethan makes sure people know he used to "hang out" with her. He makes it sound like they were a couple or something. It's a small school, and Lia's a big topic.

Most of the girls are friendly enough, but there's like this space between her and other girls. Lia's nice enough, if not aloof, and clueless as to the dynamics of our town, high school, traditions, and protocols. Or society, really. It's one of her most endearing qualities.

By Thursday I still haven't been back down to her house. Jen keeps making plans for us after practice. I tell her I need to go to Lia's to help her with something—I'm aiming for honesty—when Jen only smiles and asks what time. And that's how it ends up that Jen and I pull into Higgins' driveway, together, looking to help.

Jen turns the car off and smirks at me. "So, it's a treasure hunt?" she says for the third time, and it's all I can do not to snap.

"Yes."

"Okay, just, I'm not trying to be mean, but that's what you've been up to down here? You're helping her look for...treasure?"

I take a deep breath. I shouldn't have told her, but I'm also not sure how to handle any of this. "Look, if you're going to make fun of her, you probably shouldn't help."

Jen shakes her head. "Oh no. You can't get rid of me that easily.

I'm coming to help," she says. "There is something I've been wondering, though. You think she's scared of heights, being so high up on that pedestal you've set her on?"

I read somewhere how you can tell a person's true character by how they act under pressure. And for Jen at least, someone who's always seemed so even keel, she's coming apart at the seams.

I knock on the door but there's no answer.

"Back here," Jen says, motioning to the back, and we follow the stone path around the house where a huge pickup truck sits parked in front of the garage. Lia's sitting on the tailgate, swinging her legs, while a guy—early twenties, maybe—is hard at work on the pen I built.

Jen laughs, almost like relief in her breath, as Lia looks up, sees us, and hops down with a smile.

"Matthew, just in time."

The guy swings his head around. He's tan, muscular, a construction type with a cocky grin. My heart plummets. I swallow down the lump in my throat. "Hey, Lia."

"Hi," she says waltzing up to us. "Hi, Jen." Before Jen can say anything Lia's eyes light up. "Oh my gosh. So Linus escaped again." She looks back to the garage. "I was chasing him up and down the street—I knocked on your door—I was certain he was going to get hit by a car or lost or something awful, when..." She turns to the guy, snapping her fingers as though trying to remember his name.

He looks up and smiles again. "Ricky," he supplies.

"Right." She clicks her teeth. "*Ricky* here was working on the house up the street and the guys all hopped off the roof and so graciously helped me catch him. The little bugger was halfway down that street, the main one..."

"Fern Brook," Ricky says, being oh so helpful.

"Yeah. And so we trapped him in. He was eating out of the dumpster at the Dairy Queen. They put him in the truck and we tied him up here. Now *Ricky* is fixing up the pen, not that you didn't do a good job, but, he has all the materials and wow, what a day, huh?"

Jen takes my hand and cocks her head, watching me.

I nod. "Yeah, sounds like it."

"It was crazy. Just crazy. Ricky here is a lifesaver."

She walks over and strokes Linus's head. I take my hand back and move to get a closer look as Ricky drills in a post, really taking his time with all this free work. Lifesaver my butt, Ricky's eyes are glued to Lia's legs.

Lia baby-talks the goat. I turn, looking off to the way we came. I want to stay but I need to leave. This all feels wrong. "Well, we were just stopping by to…" I can't say it. It's awful, with Jen and this Ricky guy here, it doesn't feel right. I refuse to say treasure hunt.

But Jen has no problems with saying it. "Yeah, we were going to help you with the treasure hunt."

Lia looks over to me. My gaze drops to my feet. Ricky's drill stops. Lia recovers with a laugh. "Oh, well, I need to get Linus settled, and then there's still the wreckage of the living room, and I need to go over my lines." Lia reaches in her back pocket. "But hey, I found your phone! Well, Linus found your phone."

The cover has some nibbles on it. I laugh while Jen openly scoffs at the mention of the play. "Okay, great. Thanks. Yeah, well, we're going to take off. Nice meeting you uh, Rick-y."

Ricky gives me the head nod. Jen and I get moving toward the driveway when she takes my arm and whispers. "Well, that didn't take long."

I pull away. "What didn't take long?"

Jen's eyes shoot back toward the house. "Come on, you know. *Haha, I lost my goat, tee hee.*"

I stop. "Jen, Lia's my friend."

"What? Oh come on. No one's that innocent, Matt."

Lia's different, but Jen would never understand. "She's worried about the goat."

"Matt, are you jealous?" She studies my face. "Because you're acting kind of jealous right now."

"No, I'm not *jealous*. But I don't like you talking that way about a friend of mine."

Jen raises her hands in surrender. "Okay, okay. Can we go now?"

I DON'T SLEEP. I roll over, then over again until I'm back where I started. Jealous. Yes, I'm jealous. I'm a rotisserie of jealousy. I can't stand thinking about Ricky there saving the day. His cocky grin and the way he stared at Lia.

It's around midnight when I roll out of bed and get a drink of water. Outside, the moon is bright and gleams off of Dad's truck. I'd known Lia maybe a month the first time she convinced me to sneak out of my house. When she took me by the wrist and basically dragged me down to Greer Pond where we found Preacher Higgins, sort of sleepwalking, humming a hymn before losing his robe.

After that, we snuck out again, to check on him, then again just to go on an adventure.

And maybe I'm stuck in the past or stung with jealousy, but before I can think better of it, I'm stuffing my bare feet into my shoes and leaving the house.

The street is quiet save for the buzz of the streetlight over my head, stretching my shadow as I hustle into a jog, as though outrunning my thoughts. Like a crazy person I walk down her driveway, shaking my head because she's left the top down on the convertible. The lights are on in the house and the front door is open. My heart catches as I peek around back, where I'm flooded with relief as Ricky's truck isn't there.

Is this what I'm going to do now, spy on Lia?

Shame hits hard. What in the world am I doing? I turn to leave when I hear a voice, faintly, coming from the path, in the direction of the pond.

Might as well come clean, I'm thinking. I walk down the path, which we've cleared some now, and it's easier to navigate with the moon being so big, shining grayish on the trees.

I catch Lia's voice, with the accent, the one she always used when we were kids.

I stop at the edge of the trees, looking out to the pond. She's on the dock, a few candles at her feet, reading from a script.

"Why yes, I do love Richard, and if you cannot see that you are blind to emotion." She holds her chin up, the moonlight catching the crook of her neck. She scoffs as though talking to someone, then flings her other hand forward. "Do what you must, my conscience has been washed clean. I will die knowing I did the right thing. And that is..."

She drops the script to her side. "Matthew, what do you think?"

I come out of hiding. No sense in running away. "Well, I'd say it's a bit dramatic."

She shoots me a look, hops down from the dock. "Perfect."

I'm waiting for her to ask what I'm doing here in the middle of the night, in the woods. Instead she takes my hand. "Okay, I'm glad you're here. You take the lines of Stanley, most of them anyway. Ready?"

She thrusts the papers into my hands, takes two steps away from me, then spins around like a dueler. "Honestly, you are a horrible judge of character."

"What. I'm..." Lia nods to the papers. I search for her lines and then, "Oh, um, Rosalina, I only want what's best for you."

"Ha, what is best for me is..." She stops, bites her lip and squints in thought. Then she nods. "Ha, what is best for me is better left unsaid."

In these moments with Lia, rehearsing lines beneath the same moon that hung in the sky when were younger, it's best not to think too much and just roll with it. So I read my next line. She makes me do it again and once more after that. And then we do the entire scene again. Maybe an hour, or more, until we make our way to the house.

She's bouncing with energy, and I remind her we have to be at school in five hours.

"I know, this is an adjustment."

"What, school? Or...being back in Maycomb?" *Or just...everything.*

She waves the papers at me. "All of it. I'm really excited about theater though. I really hope I do well at the auditions."

"You will. You'll kill it, I'm sure."

We stop at her driveway, in the glow of the lights from her house. "Thanks, Matthew."

I nod when she launches into me for a hug. I hug her back, tightly, thinking about her body against mine. If anyone is watching it probably looks like she's getting ready to board a train and leave for a trip.

She pulls away and smiles. I stare into her eyes, swimming in the wonder and hope and unknown, when she nods her head. "Well, goodnight."

"Goodnight, Lia."

Chapter 16

Jen runs up to me the next morning. She's smiling and bright and way too awake for seven-thirty in the morning. "Hey."

"Hey," I say, wiping my eyes.

"You okay?" A slight frown threatens her smile.

"Yeah, just tired." A pang of guilt hits thinking about last night, when I got home after one and then stayed up staring at the ceiling with a stupid smile plastered on my face until well after three.

Jen hops in place. "Um, okay, so I was talking with Sarah, and she said Brayden said that Tyler wants to ask Lia out."

No longer tired. I retrace the path of names she mentioned. "Huh?"

"Like, a triple date. Doesn't that sound fun? Unless, you know, Lia and Ricky have plans." She nudges me.

I don't laugh. "Yeah, okay." What am I saying?

Jen is thrilled with this development. She takes my hand. "I was thinking Friday, after the game. We could all go to Porter Grill and then maybe hang out somewhere. See how it goes."

"You don't think that's weird?"

"*Weird*. Why would it be weird?"

"No, it wouldn't. Yeah. Sure."

She shoots me a look. "*OhhKay*. So I'll tell Sarah. Let's find Tyler and Lia at lunch and see how it goes. I'm so excited. Yay."

She gives me a quick peck on the cheek and dashes off to find Sarah. I'm left wondering what just happened.

I get through Lit, wander through the rest of the morning, and by lunch, having set my tray down at the table, Jen and Sarah are all

"Where is she?" While Brayden and the ever so hopeful Tyler Parks give me head nods.

"I think she's..." I nod to the doors leading to the courtyard outside. "Hang on."

I set off after Lia, trying not to put too much thought into what I'm doing. She's playing frisbee golf with a pack of freshmen. I laugh, because these kids must think they've hit the lottery, this beautiful upperclassman hanging out with them.

"Hey, um, Lia."

She turns and smiles at me. I wonder how every single time her smile can have such an effect on my heart, chest, throat, breath. She shoves one of the freshmen playfully. "Hey, Matthew. Watch, Jose thinks he can take me, but he can't."

She flexes at him. I laugh, again struck by the thought, *Why don't we just leave?* Hop in the Chrysler and hit the parkway. But behind me sits the cafeteria, and this stupid idea of setting Lia up on a date.

"So, um, hey can I talk to you?"

"Oh, sure," she says. She turns to the kids and wags a finger. "I'll be back."

She skips over to me, her bracelets bouncing with her strides. "So what's up? Did you finally realize how much better it is to be outside instead of at some stupid lunch table?" She stands so close I can feel her breath, her eyes some kind of goldish-green-blue fascination.

"Um, no. Actually, I was hoping you might uh, eat with us today."

"Oh," she says, curling her lip.

"It's, well, there's someone who wants to..." I look off, past the fence and the trees, to the mountains in the distance. "Someone who wants to meet you."

She straightens, assumes a British accent. "Oh, I should feel honored, yeah?"

I laugh. "Um, sure."

She takes my arm in hers. "Well, lead the way."

I sort of want to go hide in a bathroom stall. Jen has rounded up

Sarah and Brayden, who stand around as Tyler, his hair gelled and set in place, awaits with a cocky smile.

Tyler Parks is popular, well-off, on the tennis team, and generally well-liked. He drives a bright red Jeep, dated Hope Haley last year. But now, as he sees us walk in and starts wiping at his hair, it's clear he's got his sights set on Lia. It feels like the entire cafeteria is staring at us.

"Hi, Lia," Jen says, all bubbly and friendly. "I'm so glad you came to join us."

"Yeah," Lia sits next to me and immediately leans over and steals a french fry from my tray. Jen watches us carefully.

"So, Lia. I think you've met Sarah, and this is Brayden. And this is Tyler Parks."

"Hey, Lia," he says leaning over. "Nice to meet you."

Lia smiles. "Hi."

I feel like I've eaten a tray of rocks and they're all sinking in my stomach. Outside, the sun is shining. I shouldn't have dragged her in here.

"So," Jen says, looking around and making everything worse than it already is. "As you probably already know, Friday is the first football game. We're all going to cheer Matt on, and we were wondering if you would like to join us." She points to Sarah and Brayden.

Tyler clears his throat. "Yeah, I was hoping you'd let me show you around?"

All eyes on Lia, who looks at me then back to the group. "Oh, well I'm new to the school, but I've been here before. Actually, Matthew and I used to get in all sorts of trouble, didn't we, Matthew?"

I smile. "I wouldn't say all sorts."

"Oh, come on, at Sweeney's? Remember when you knocked everything over? And then at the pond, when you…"

Tyler's smile drops.

Jen frowns. She clears her throat. "Well, anyway, the game. What do you say?"

Lia looks at Jen, then to Sarah to Brayden and back to Tyler as she puts it all together. "Oh, well."

When she looks at me directly, I think about last night. Rehearsing lines. On the dock. And now, here at school, I can't summon the words to tell her the truth. To tell everyone the truth. All I can do is watch as all the hope and flash and memories vanish from her eyes. She turns back to Jen. "Yeah sure, okay."

Chapter 17

By the time I get to Lia's on Wednesday, I find her on the porch. Linus is not in his pen but roaming in the yard. Lia's reading over her lines and doesn't seem to notice when I approach. It could be because she has a cat lying on her chest.

I shake my head. "You got a cat?"

She strokes the cat, doesn't say hello or even acknowledge my presence. I take a seat on the old metal chair, the same chairs Higgins used to sit on and watch as I'd cut his lawn—which needs mowing. "How are your lines coming along?"

She looks up and smiles. "Good." She looks down to the cat. Black with white paws. "This is Fremont."

"When uh, when did you get a cat?"

"Fremont. Today."

So many questions. "So I was thinking about the treasure. What about the garage? That's where the car was. Have you thought to look in the trunk?"

She shrugs, still patting the cat, looking over the lines. "No."

Another look at the high grass and with a sigh, I get up. Only then does Lia lower the lines. "Where are you going?"

I gesture to the yard. "Well, the grass needs mowing, and you're busy, so..."

She looks out to the yard. "It's why I have a goat."

I laugh despite myself. What I really want to talk about is the stupid date thing, but I don't know how to bring that up. "Lia, look..."

Before I can finish she's on her feet. She opens the door and sets the cat inside. She slaps my chest with the script. "Oh, I have a surprise."

"It's not the cat?"

"Nope." Her eyes flash. "Want to see?"

I follow her down the trail. She's moving fast, and I have to jog to keep up. We get around the bend and to the pond, where she scans things and then hops in place. "There."

I follow her direction to the back edge of the pond where there's a family of ducks. "Where did…?"

She walks carefully to the dock, looking over her shoulder with a whisper. "You have to be quiet while they get used to the pond. Shhh."

I edge up beside her, and the ducks don't seem to mind. I count six of them.

Her eyes go wide. "Aren't they the cutest?"

"Yeah. But Lia, are you really turning this place into a farm? Or a zoo?"

She smiles, her gaze never leaving the ducks. "Farm. Zoo. Who knows? But I may get some chickens. Wouldn't that be fun?"

We sit there, watching the ducks swim and preen and flutter about. Lia toes the water in the pond and then leans back. "So what's up with setting me up on a date?"

"Oh, that. Yeah, um, I don't know. Jen said Tyler…" It sounds so trivial here at the pond, with the ducks. With her. She waits and then looks off. "I don't know. You don't have to go."

She looks back. "Well, I want to go to your game, I still don't have any solid proof you play football. I'll have to see it to believe it. So I'll go."

"What do you mean, *you still don't have proof*? I just left practice."

"So you say."

I turn to her and she giggles. I nudge her with my arm and she nudges me back. Is it cheating, the way I feel? Yes, I think so. If my thoughts are any indication, I'm a two-timing slimeball.

The ducks make a noise, like they're not happy with our

intrusion. Lia's hair falls over her face. She slings it back. "Okay, so you think the treasure is in the trunk?"

"I only said it might be a place to check."

She bites her lip and looks to the trail. "Should we go check?"

We get to the driveway, and Lia takes the keys from the ignition. "Okay," she jingles them my way. "If we find a body, I'm blaming you."

I laugh, but my breath catches as she fiddles with the key chain. Could there really be a treasure? Or am I just caught up in Lia's imaginative pull? She puts the key in, then sighs, and I tell her to try it the other way and her eyes light up as something clicks. She looks at me, her eyebrows cocked.

I laugh. "You are so dramatic."

"Well good, maybe I'll get the part. Okay, ready?"

I roll my eyes.

She lifts the trunk, which is big enough for a body but contains nothing but a big fat spare tire. Her shoulders drop. I lean in the trunk. "Maybe it's..."

She sets her hand on her hip. "Man, you really had me thinking there was going to be a treasure."

"I just thought it was a place to look."

She sits on the edge of the trunk. I sit beside her and the car squeaks under our weight. "Lia, not trying to be a downer, but there's probably not a treasure, you know."

She stares at her feet. "Yeah, I know. I just liked the thought of it. I don't really want or need money, but...wouldn't it be cool to find something like that?"

I nod. "Yeah."

We sit there for a second. The two of us at the edge of the trunk. I'm enjoying the quiet comfort between us as a breeze falls over us. Then I realize Lia is crying.

At first I think it's a laugh when I feel her shaking and trembling, but when I look at her, her cheeks are wet.

"Lia?"

She covers her face, and I set my arm around her. She falls into me with a sob. And I'm wondering what's going on but I stop myself from asking, because, the empty trunk, the big house, all the land, and a new school. It's a lot.

Lia lifts her head to pull away but doesn't make it. She sniffles, sets her cheek against my chest. "I feel so alone."

I start to say a million things, but if nothing else, Lia has taught me that sometimes it's better to listen. She wipes her eyes, fingers the dog tag, but she never lets me go.

"My mom is in jail. My dad is dead. *Higgins* is dead. It just feels like sometimes, there's nowhere to go. Nowhere at all."

I pull her closer. With Lia, it's hard to tell what she's thinking most of the time. She's so good at being...Lia, that it's easy to forget what she's going through.

"I'm so sorry, Lia."

She moves away and wipes her eyes. "No, it's nothing you've done, Matthew. I just," she laughs. "I'm still breaking down in front of you. I wonder if that's a good thing or a bad thing?"

"Lia."

She shakes her head, wipes her eyes, and gets to her feet, smiling through the tears, forcing happiness onto her face as she leaps off the trunk and gazes out to the yard. "Where is that stupid goat?"

I don't want to worry about Linus. I'm worried about Lia being alone. I want to hug her close again.

"Linus."

I get off the car, shut the trunk. Lia walks out to the high grass, her hair clumped over to one side, her legs set and her shoulders square. She's back, her little moment of weakness over. She's Lia again.

And so I follow her to the yard, looking for the goat, my shirt still wet with her tears.

Chapter 18

Coach Cutright tells us we're not ready. We're going to get creamed if we go into tomorrow night's game against Ellison with such a casual mindset.

I think if he had it his way we wouldn't have started school. It's a distraction. The classes, the teachers, the girls, damn it. We need to be focused. Now run.

We run laps. And with each thick, humid breath I think about Lia crying yesterday. I wonder how her ducks are faring, if Linus is behaving. If she's feeling alone.

The last thing I'm focused on is the actual game tomorrow night. The stupid date? Lia and Tyler? Yes, I'm extremely focused on that part. It sends electric pulses through my chest every time I think about it.

By lap three Coach tells us to pick it up. I need to be honest with Jen about how I feel. Even if I don't know exactly what I'm feeling, Lia needs me and that's enough. Lap four and I'm completely drenched in sweat. Either way, no matter what happens with Lia, at least my conscience would be clear.

Coach brings us in. We line up in formation. I drop a pass, and Coach blasts his whistle. "Crosby, what was that?"

I shrug. Coach shakes his head. It's that kind of day. We line up and I make the next catch. While I'm not a superstar, this was supposed to be my breakout year. I've always been solid. That's what the coaches call me. Big. Solid. Reliable. Hard working. I've got what it takes to play DIII ball.

Thing is, I'm bored.

Football used to be enough, but I had nothing else to do. Now I want to go treasure hunting. I want to help clean out Higgins' house. I want to wander through the woods down to the pond. I want to know what goes on in Lia's head. This has happened before.

Three years ago to be exact.

I was on the baseball team with Ethan. I was terrible, but it was something to do. Lia came along and showed me everything I was missing. I quit. My dad was not happy. And now, as Coach has us line up, threatening miles more laps if we don't get our stuff together, I know if I quit now, quit on the team before the first game of the season, I'd have more than my dad to answer to, I'd let down my teammates and the entire school.

So I get my stuff together. I make the catches. I focus. Big. Solid. Reliable.

On Friday Jen is so excited she could pop. The school buzzes with energy, the big game. Ellison High is coming to town.

I drift through my morning classes, until lunch, when I skip the cafeteria and find Lia outside. But Tyler has beat me to it.

"Hey," he says to me. I turn, startled. Tyler smiles, standing at a tree, watching Lia with a hunter's gleam in his eyes. All that's missing is a scope and a gun. It makes me want to punch him in the face.

Lia argues with a freshman about the placement of a frisbee. Tyler grins at me. "Big night, tonight."

I can't tell if he means the stupid game or the stupid date. "Yeah."

"So uh, what is she doing out here, anyway?" he says with a laugh. Then, before I can think of an answer, he leans closer, talking under his breath. "Dude, it's crazy. I'm not usually down with the brown, you know?" He nods Lia's way. "But I'll make an exception here."

I turn to him, a hot rashy anger climbing up my neck to my face. "What did you say?"

He takes a step back as though I misheard him. "What? No, I just... Look, bro, I didn't mean it in a bad way."

I take another step toward him, my fists balling up, when Lia calls out. "Matthew, hey."

I stop. Lia gives her discs to one of her little friends, says she'll be back.

"Hey, guys," she says, approaching, looking us over.

I step back.

Tyler steps forward. "Hi, Lia."

I can't unlock my jaw to get words out. Lia smiles at him but glances again at me. I'm quaking with anger, and it's getting harder not to punch him or tell her to get away from this guy.

She hops to a stop and sets her hands on her hips. "Well, you guys want to play?"

"Oh." Tyler laughs like it's a big joke. His cheeks are flushed, enough to match his little pink Polo shirt. I'm probably flushed too, because this pretty boy tennis player saying that stuff about Lia. He looks over to me. "You think Matty here is up for the big game tonight?"

Lia looks me over. Suddenly my stupid jersey feels fraudulent. She takes the sleeve in her hands and smiles. "Shiny. You look good in blue."

Tyler frowns. A frisbee comes flying over our heads and we duck in unison. Lia squeals.

"Okay, who threw it!"

They all point to each other. Lia smiles at us. "Kids, right? What are you going to do?"

Tyler goes to say something witty, I'm sure, but Lia dashes off for the frisbee. Again he asks what she's doing. But I'm done faking it. I turn to him and get in his face. "I'm going to say this once. Don't ever talk about her like that again."

Tyler throws his hands up. "Bro, relax, man. Okay?" He looks around. "Aren't you with Jen? I thought you were okay with this?"

I take a breath, try to put on a good face as Lia comes darting past us.

"That's it, someone's going to get it." She's wearing some sort of capri pants, a loose blouse, her hair hangs over her face, and I'm pretty sure no one else could pull this look off. The freshmen boys are wide-eyed and in love.

And maybe they're not the only ones.

AFTER SCHOOL THAT DAY, Jen insists we go by the store. She says her grandpa wants to talk with me. I tell her it's okay, but she won't have it. We walk in and the old timers light up at the sight of my jersey. Pride fills their eyes. *Go get 'em tonight* and all that.

We find Mr. Yearly in the back, struggling with a bag of mulch. Instinctively I walk over and help him. He thanks me, wipes his hands, and looks me over.

"Hiya, Matt. Thanks a lot." He nods at his granddaughter. "Jenny, dear."

Jen says hello, and Mr. Yearly asks me to come out to the loading dock. I already know he's going to offer me my job back, but I think he'd like me to grovel some.

"So," he says, fiddling with an invoice. A pallet of mulch sits between us. The dock smells strong of fertilizer, and if I'm being honest, it's nice to be back—the smells, the breeze, the soft swoosh of traffic from the main road.

"Big game tonight, no?"

I nod. I really, really don't want to do this right now. But if nothing else, my dad has always taught me to look a man in the eyes, show my elders respect. Even when it's awkward. Like this.

"Ellison's got that fullback, think you boys can bring him down?"

I go through the motions, talking ball with him. "Yeah, sure we can. We'll try. Going to be a fight to the end."

I almost cringe saying it. We do this for five or ten minutes before he straightens a few boxes and looks me over. "Look, you know I'm protective about my granddaughter, and when you ran off, I assumed the worst."

It's all I can do to stand there and nod and take it. He keeps on for a while, until a truck backs into the dock and I offer to help load up, off the clock, whatever to get this over with.

He turns to me, sets a hand on my shoulder. "Let's get you back in here on Saturday for your shift. How's that?"

"Yeah, sure," I say, lifting the first bag of mulch from the pallet. "Thanks."

Mr. Yearly waves his hands. "No, no, Mr. Kemp can get that. You rest up for tonight."

Chapter 19

On the field for warm ups, as the sun settles over the mountains, heat and humidity still grip the stadium. While football is a fall sport, it's early September and summer has no plans on leaving.

Looking out to Ellison, they're as big as advertised. Last year they went to regionals, and, like us got knocked out in the first round. But they were young and most of their core is back.

Now we're the young team. I'm one of only eight seniors on our squad. No matter, after our strong showing last year everyone expects us to break through this year. Now we have to live up to expectations, focus on what we do best. But I can't stop looking up at the stands.

Every time I think of Lia and Tyler—what he said—them sitting with Jen and Sarah and Brayden, it blasts me with a sort of runaway panic, and I have to remind myself Lia's a tough girl and can fend for herself.

James and Austin slap my helmet, shove me as they get hyped and ready to hit someone. Coach stalks our end of the field, clapping and whistling and telling us, *That's it, that's it.*

He calls me over to him. "Matt, what's going on? I need you to be here with us tonight."

I nod. "Yeah, I'm here, Coach."

He looks me over, lowers his voice. "I don't have to tell you how big this game is, do I? You're a senior, one of my leaders. I'm expecting more from you this year, got it?"

"Got it, Coach."

We get to the locker room and Coach paces and gears up for his pregame speech. He must have read a few more books over the summer, done some leadership conference, because he's got a few new cliches sprinkled in with his usual routine.

By the time we get out, the crowd has arrived, and the sun is a little lower. It's still hot, maybe hotter than it was. I tell myself I'm ready.

I am not ready.

Ellison kicks off and the entire team follows the ball in the air. I glance up from the sidelines, look off, and spot Jen. She waves and smiles and Sarah and Brayden are laughing and there's Tyler, next to Lia and leaning to say something into her ear. Lia looks about as out of place at a football game as a wild bird who's flown into a house.

Tyler points at me and Lia perks up. She waves, and I smile and wave back. I start thinking about Linus and hope she's put him in his pen so he won't get away, when Coach Rucker, our offensive coordinator, reminds me there's a game on the field.

By the time the offense takes the field, I'm convinced I've pushed everything out of my mind. I'm ready. I'm not thinking about Tyler over there flirting with Lia. What if his charm works? What if she likes him? What if she agrees to go out with him again? What if she invites him down to the pond?

I allow myself a quick glance, and again he's leaning over to her, no doubt explaining the game, and who knows what else.

"Matty, want to join us?" Austin says as the huddle breaks. He points for me to go out wide, he motions, *No, wider. Come on, Matty, get out there.* The ball snaps and the fullback takes the end but I miss a block and he's chopped down.

The guys are looking my way. I clap my hands, get into the motions. Tyler is up there pointing to something—the freaking tennis pro—and by then the ball has snapped and I'm lost. We punt.

Ellison scores on a deep ball, which, even though I'm not playing cornerback, apparently since I missed the block, it's entirely my fault. Austin throws his helmet, something he never does because he's usually the one encouraging the guys and being a leader and all that.

The defense is pissed, too. It's early, but we're off to a terrible start. It already seems like a disaster.

"What in the hell?" James stomps around, the defense guys all smacking shoulder pads, huffing and growling at each other. I look off, shaking my head at how stupid everyone is acting when Aiden, our running back, gets in my face, chopping his hand into his palm for emphasis. "Matt. Get your head in this game!"

On the very next possession, I get beat on the blitz and Austin gets creamed. Again we punt and it's more of the same. No one comes near me until Coach Rucker approaches. I hold back an eye roll as he takes the calm approach.

"Don't let it get to you. This next series I'm going right back to you, okay? So be ready."

Our defense forces a stop. Ellison punts the ball back to us, and we're down 7-0 and I'm telling myself not to look up to the stands, but Tyler and Lia aren't there. It's just Jen and Sarah, whispering, Brayden looking much too serious.

I try to look without turning my helmet. Did they go to the concession stand? Was Lia bored and talked Tyler into leaving? Where did they go?

Austin barks out the call, he glances at me and I know what it means. I set my mouthpiece in my mouth and decide it's time to make a play, a big play.

I choose my route. The stunt is for me to drop back like I'm going to block then shoot out for a quick pass. We've done it a million times. Wait, break, five yards, turn and catch. But for some reason, tonight I want more. I want to make the catch, turn, and blast my way downfield.

The ball leaves the center's hand. Austin turns to Aiden and I backpedal like I'm pulling to block for the sweep. I wait, wait, then go.

I release. Austin sells the fake, then, as soon as I turn, he puts the ball where it needs to go. I reach out, as I've done so many times before, make the catch and drop for the first down. But this time I turn and take a step, and with that next step comes a spark of light. A clack of helmets, then everything goes black.

The first time I kissed Lia we were on the dock. She'd just shoved me into the pond, and then I'd repaid her by pulling her in when she tried to help me out. By the time we got back on the dock, we were soaked, dripping wet, and Lia looked at me and said I could kiss her.

It was there, in those woods at Higgins' house, where our lips met and I was changed forever.

"Matt!"

"Yo, Matt, you there?"

I blink to find six or seven helmets leaning over me. Wide eyes, mouthpieces, sweat. Coach is somewhere above them as Amy, the athletic trainer, yells for everyone to make room. It's quiet in the stadium. I'm suddenly aware that the game has stopped and everyone is watching, my parents included. Austin stands a few steps back.

"Matthew."

Then there's Lia, her face a mess of worry. My thoughts feel heavy like mush, and I can't tell if it's real. Is she really down here? How?

Again, Amy barks for everyone to give me room, but Lia kneels, leans over me. Amy once again tells her to give me space. I nod to Lia, who's not crying but looks ready to start.

"Hey, I'm okay." I try to lift my head but Amy catches me.

"Matt, lay back." Then, louder. "Can someone get her off the field, please?"

"Lia, hey. I'm okay."

Austin helps Lia as she backs away, the lights glimmering over her hair. "Are you sure?"

The play. I released, the ball came. I caught it. But the linebacker hit me like a freight train. And then I remember something else. The ball. "I fumbled."

Coach grimaces. They all surround me. Everyone tells me it's okay. I lose Lia in the light, the bodies. Then she's gone and I wonder if it was real. Or how she rushed the field, then again it's not exactly the Super Bowl.

The bodies part. The sky looks purple beyond the stadium lights. I blink and sit up. Amy runs some tests and declares me okay to walk off the field but I've had a concussion and I'm done for the night.

The crowd cheers for me as I leave the field.

Chapter 20

After protocols and testing in the locker room, I return to the sidelines. A few more cheers in the crowd, some pats on the back, but most of the focus returns to the game. Ellison is up by ten and it's a night to forget. I've allowed a tackle for a loss, a sack, and I've fumbled the ball. And I'm trying to care, but it's hard. I really just want to leave.

Jen has come down to the front row. She's crying, but at the same time annoyed that Lia made such "a spectacle" of being on the field.

Speaking of Lia, she's gone. So is Tyler. Mom and Dad come down to the track. Mom looks pale, her eyes puffy. Dad is grim. I tell them I'm fine, but it's already looking like I'll miss next week due to protocols. I can't believe I fumbled.

Ellison tacks on another field goal, and their experience pays off as we sputter again on offense and they start running down the clock with the running game.

I'm able to skip out on post-game activities due to my injury, even as I'm feeling okay, maybe a little woozy, but nothing major.

Mom demands I come home where she can keep an eye on me. When I tell Jen, she sighs. "So much for date night."

Sarah and Brayden wait at Jen's car. But it gives me a chance to ask about Lia without raising suspicion. Jen shrugs, rolls her eyes. "She said she wanted to go home. You know, don't take this the wrong way, but maybe theater will be her thing after all. What a drama queen."

I don't have the energy to argue with her. Four months nearly, we've been together. She's always been sweet, thoughtful, and our mutual interests got us through the low points. But now, as the burn leaves my chest and my face goes hot, I'm not sure what I ever saw in her.

"What, why are you looking at me like that?"

"Like what?"

"Like you hate me."

"I'm not. Look, Jen..." I sigh. "I can't right now, I'm sorry. I'm just tired."

"Okay," she says, sliding up next to me. I can tell she's still upset about our plans, but I didn't exactly intend to get knocked out on the field. It's a little surprising how little it bothers me. The loss, not playing, being out next week.

Jen runs a hand down my side. "Well, I'll give you a ride home. I can tell Sarah that they'll have to go without us."

In the car, Sarah goes on about something the cheerleaders did. Braydon is hungry, and Jen raises her eyebrows and asks what Tyler and Lia are doing.

"I thought she went home," I say.

"Yeah, bet they did go home," Braydon says with a smile. Sarah gives him a playful slap.

I turn around too fast and the world spins. I blink hard. "What's that supposed to mean?"

Brayden's smile drops. "What? I'm just saying, doesn't she have her own place?"

Jen closes her eyes and exhales. "It's a little annoying how you're always defending her."

"She's my friend. And is that cool, to assume she wanted to take some dude home?"

The car gets quiet. My head rumbles. We snake through the parking lot, the headlights and tail lights doing their best to aggravate the dull ache in my head. A month ago, weeks, I'd been so ready for this. Senior year, the first big game. The world in my hands. Now, it seems pathetic.

Brayden and Sarah cuddle up in the back, whispering and

pawing at each other. Jen taps the wheel, plays with the radio, and otherwise ignores me. A chime in the backseat.

Brayden's phone glows. He laughs. "Yeah, I guess you were right, Matty."

I start to turn but can't make the trip. Jen checks the rearview mirror. Brayden holds up his phone. "Uh, Tyler said he'll wait for us at Matt's place." He chuckles. "Said that chick is nuts."

I restrain my smile from cracking open. But Jen must feel it as she cuts her eyes to me before we pull out onto the main drag. "That should make you happy."

Sure enough, Jen pulls down my street and there's Tyler's Jeep at the curb. She turns into my driveway. I get out and steady myself against the roof as Tyler pops out of his Jeep.

Brayden laughs. "You bailed?"

Tyler looks at me. "You okay, man? That was a nasty hit."

"I'm good, just...a headache."

He nods. "Cool. That's why I play tennis. Anyway, okay, Lia's all freaking out about our boy here. I mean, she did rush the field and all. So she wanted to go home, and I was like, okay cool. I'm thinking... never mind." He glances at me and changes gears. "I don't know, but I get to her house and I walk her to the door, when this freaking goat comes out of nowhere and rams me in the ass."

"A goat?" Sarah repeats, as though she can't fathom.

Jen rolls her eyes.

"Yeah, a freaking goat. Like an attack dog or some shit." He slaps his butt. "Thing came out of nowhere and got me right here. I'm like what the... So I kick at it, to chase it off you know, and this chick lights into me. She's all like, 'don't you touch Linus.' And I'm like who the hell is Linus?"

Brayden doubles over. "Linus the goat."

I'm chuckling, too, but for different reasons, until I look across the roof where Jen is glaring at me. Tyler continues on about the goat, about Lia slapping him, kicking him out, about getting a rabies shot, while Sarah shakes her head as though it's the craziest thing anyone's ever said. And maybe it's my head or because I'm not really thinking about it, I say, "Lots of people have goats, it's not exactly a big deal."

The laughter stops. Sarah looks at Brayden. Jen's mouth parts but she doesn't say anything. Tyler laughs. "Yeah, farmers do, but...I don't know. Are you guys hungry?"

Sarah and Brayden say they are. Jen only watches me. "Well, apparently I'm not invited in, so I'll leave."

I turn to Jen, about to ask her to come in, but I don't feel like fighting or watching her pout. I just want to lay around and not think about anything.

Brayden looks up from his phone. "Get well, man."

"Thanks, guys." I look at Jen. "I'll call you tomorrow?"

She shrugs. "Whatever."

I head for the front door. Brayden gets in the Jeep with Tyler and I hear them laughing, about Lia, goats, and whatever else. Sarah gets in with Jen to comfort and support and call me a jerk. I throw a wave their way and go inside.

Mom paces the floor in front of me. She knew this would happen, it's why she didn't want me playing football in the first place. Dad is much calmer, but keeps a careful gaze on me. I sit, tell them what I remember.

"I don't know, I just wanted to make a play..." I shake my head.

Dad looks at Mom. I look from Dad to Mom then back to Dad. "What?"

Dad's chest swells as he takes a breath. "Coach says you were distracted. Weren't in the game. Been distracted in practice all week."

I shift in my seat. "When did he say all that?"

He wipes his forehead. "He waved us down as you were leaving. He thought it was something we should know."

"Oh, okay. Not, *how is he? Tell him to take care.* None of that?"

"He said to get some rest. You can do walk-throughs at practice but no pads for a week. That's the thinking right now anyway."

Mom takes a deep breath through her nose. "I don't care if he doesn't play at all."

Dad looks at Mom. "What about the scholarship? We've got two partials as it is."

Mom waves him off. "His grades are fine, we can figure it out. This isn't helping."

Slowly, I get to my feet. "I'm going to bed."

Mom reaches for me. "I'm supposed to keep a watch on you tonight. How is Jen, anyway? She seemed awfully shaken up about you."

I shrug. "I think she's...over it."

Chapter 21

I replay it in my head. What happened, how I could have made the catch and dropped down. We only needed a few yards. I have a lamp on, then it's off. I go in and out of sleep, and Mom is good about checking on me every two hours. Too good, it's annoying.

At some point, maybe she falls asleep, she stops knocking and asking how I'm doing. I blink in the dark, still thinking about the game, Jen, until I'm not. I'm at the edge of sleep when I feel a soft hand on my face.

"Shh."

Definitely not Mom. The hand lingers, a warm palm on my cheek. I blink, and I catch a hint of vanilla. And then her body is beside me.

"Lia?"

She nuzzles against my neck. "I just wanted to check on you."

Sparks shoot through my head. A firework display of color in the dark. I push up on one elbow. "How did you get in?"

I feel her smile. "The window. I'm quite sneaky, you don't remember?"

"I was looking for you, after the game." Her hair brushes my face and it hits me fully. I'm in bed with Lia. Again she nuzzles herself into my neck.

"They made me leave. I really didn't want to hang around anyway. I'm sorry, but don't expect me to come to anymore games, okay?"

I set my head back, still groggy but wide awake, exploding with hope yet there's a weight on my chest shoving me back, heavy.

"I heard Linus was mean to your date."

She snorts, covers it with her hand. "Oh my goodness," she whispers. "Yes. Linus was very rude, to say the least."

Then I'm giggling too, and we're being loud. "We have to be quiet, my mom keeps checking on me."

Two hands take my face. "Hey, I was really scared tonight. You were lying on the field like a lump. I'm sorry if I embarrassed you. I took off over the railing, I wasn't thinking. I'm not very good at high school, I don't think."

I take her wrist, caress her arm. Our fingers intertwine. "It's okay. I didn't want you there anyway. To be honest, I didn't want to be there so much myself."

She pulls away. "Really?"

I nod. The window is open, my curtains parted, allowing a slice of the streetlight into my room. I can make out her hair, her wide eyes. The silhouette of her lips when she turns her head.

"Yeah, I don't know. My head hasn't been in the game recently. Coach knows it, I guess everyone knows it, now."

She snorts. "Your head is the last thing you need *in the game*. Smashing into one another for a few hours while the crowd cheers you on? It's all rather barbaric."

Only Lia. Things get quiet, and we lie together for a minute, something buzzing between us. My heart has picked up and thumps in my ears. I wonder if she can feel it. My childhood dream lies next to me, against me, a mess of crazy notions and adventures.

I think back to Lia in the stands with Tyler. How it drove me crazy. I really have to talk to Jen, come clean, suck it up and let her be angry with me. And I will, but for now, I turn to Lia and say, "I really want to do more treasure hunting."

She lifts up, over me, smiling like a loon. "I was so hoping you'd say that. I have some ideas, I think—"

Two knocks tap the door before it cracks open. Lia ducks under the covers in an instant. Mom peeks in.

"How are you doing, sweetie?"

"Uh." Lia's hair tickles my arm. I'm acutely aware that she's against me, her warm breaths, as Mom is asking me...what is she asking me? Oh, right. "I'm okay, Mom. Really."

She nods, half asleep. "Okay, do you need some water, Tylenol, or..."

"I'm good, Mom. Thank you."

She starts to pull away, but then, "I've been thinking about it, Matt. How you need to be honest about your feelings with Jen."

"Mom." *Seriously.* Now?

"I know, but honey it's obvious that your feelings are elsewhere, since Lia came back you've been a mess, the least you—"

"Mom, I'm really tired," I say, blinking, glad she can't see the red hot panic on my face, the heat of my skin against Lia in my bed.

"Okay, okay. I'm sorry, but...think about it, okay?"

"Mmm, hmm. Yep."

She pulls the door shut and Lia pops up. She only stares at me. "Do you?"

"Do I?"

"Matthew, do you?"

I think I know what she means and the answer is yes, it's been yes. And when Lia lowers her head and our lips touch, it's gentle and soft. Then I'm kissing her back and my body flushes until she pulls away, wipes her hair to the side.

She smiles then kisses me again. And it's like when we were younger but it's so much more—it's soft and quick, and then it's longer, deeper, and more meaningful. And when my arms wrap around her sides and her hands reach for me, from my chin to my chest to my ribs, I'm vaguely aware that my mom was just at the door and I know this is bad but kissing Lia is all I've been dreaming of for three years and now it's happening exactly where I dreamed it.

THE NEXT MORNING I wake up alone. I close my eyes, breathe in the scent of my sheets and my pillows and smell the traces of her in the dark. I sit up on my elbows, looking to my window and wondering.

Mom knocks softly and I jump. She cracks the door and shoots me a look. "How are you, dear?"

"Good, um." I rub my head, glancing to the floor, subtly searching for any trace of Lia. Did she really come in my room last night? Through the window? We were kissing, I'm sure of it, right?

Mom reads my confusion as grogginess. "I'm sorry, well, I fell asleep and didn't get to check in on you."

"I'm fine, Mom. Really."

She continues to study me carefully. Then she smiles. "Well, this is one way to get out of helping your father on his weekend chores. He's already at Lowe's."

I lay back. "Busted. I totally faked the whole thing because I was not about to set fence posts all day."

Mom smiles. "I made breakfast."

Once she's gone I look around again, searching for a ghost. Then I flop back down and smile, reliving the kisses in the dark, the warmth of Lia's body in my arms. I'm smiling until I think about Jen—then it's all I can do to live with myself.

What kind of horrible person does that? I find a shirt and get dressed, knowing I can't push it off any longer. I have to tell her.

I gobble down breakfast. Mom goes out on errands but she's still worried about me, judging by the six text messages she sends. And then I see the seventh.

We need to talk.

Jen. And we do need to talk, but right now it's ten o'clock on a Saturday and yes, I'm a terrible person, horrible person. And we will have that uncomfortable talk, but first, I'm walking down the street.

Lia's door is open. I call through the screen. "Lia?" I walk in. "I hope you're dressed this time."

She calls down the hallway. "Do you?"

I laugh. "Um... Where are you?"

"In here."

I find her in a bedroom halfway down the hall. An office, with books stuffed in the shelves lining the walls, boxes of records spilling all over the bed. Today's outfit is some sort of loose floral blouse that I'm thinking must have belonged to Judith. The cut-off jean shorts not so much.

She looks back at me. "Did you know Mr. Higgins gambled?"

I shrug, shake my head. Painted. Preached. Gambled. Why not?

She nods. "And he was really good at it, apparently."

I take a seat beside her on the bed, the springs sinking under my weight. "I didn't know people could be good at gambling."

"Well, he was." She smiles, then the smile drops. "How are you feeling?"

"Good. Okay, I guess." I stop myself from saying more. Mainly, *Was last night real?*

Lia's smile returns. She sorts through books, holding up a yellowed paper. "Horses mostly. Dogs, too. And he won a lot. I had no idea. Look, five-hundred dollars here, a couple thousand there."

I look over the entries, when Lia looks at me with a smile. "You know what this means right?"

"Don't say it."

She leaps off the bed and takes my hands. "Treasure. Treasure. Treasure. Treasure."

"What about bank accounts?"

"Nope, Sterling has been through that with me. Remember? I have a trust fund?"

"Oh."

"Yeah, but that's for mostly the utilities, taxes, and boring stuff. But this," she walks to the desk. "None of this is mentioned."

"Hmm."

"Want to know why?"

I roll my eyes. She points to the window and whispers dramatically. "Because it's buried out there."

"Let me guess what we're doing today?"

She looks me over, head to toe. "*We?* Oh, there's a *we* now?"

My face warms up and she lets me suffer, staring at me with wide eyes until I backtrack and stammer "No, I just mean..."

Lia tilts her head to the side, a hand on her hip as she waits me out.

I try again, then once more, to put a sentence together. "Lia, look. I'm not sure, I thought..."

"Ha!" She jumps back with a huge smile. I lower my head as Lia busts out laughing. She folds over then comes flying back up, having a great time. She leans back, rocking on her heels. "Oh, I had you good. So good. Now do you think I'll get the part?"

My gaze stays on my feet. "I have no doubt."

Before I can get mad at her she crosses the small room and closes in on me. She takes my hands in hers. "Of course you can help me. There will, however, be a ninety-eight to two percent split on whatever we find."

"Sounds generous."

"Oh, it is. And two percent of anything is more than you deserve for making me hang out with *Tyler*. Now come on."

She wheels around and out the door. I look over the receipts and notes, the yellowed cards filled with Higgins' numbers and cursive. Suddenly the day is brighter. I stuff the Jen thing to the back of my mind, and I don't think about football or much of anything else.

Because I'm going treasure hunting.

Chapter 22

Lia thinks we should abandon the pines and focus on the garage. I remind her that was my idea all along, but she won't hear it. We march around back, and the sun is out and it's warm and I'm wondering if we're going to talk about last night, but she's lost in the mission.

Her old Honda sits in the back with the windows down. I look over the Georgia plates, the tires sagging low, almost flat. "So, what's the plan with this?"

"What?"

I nod to the Honda. She frowns. "I don't know. We've been through so much together."

I imagine her sleeping in the car, tapping on the steering wheel on the highway, belting out songs. Or maybe since it's her mom's car she feels the need to hang on to it.

Before I can look away from it, Lia's already tearing into the garage. Boxes line the wall to the back where there's a few old Coke machines, bikes, push mowers, rakes, dusty canvas awnings, and all sorts of other junk.

"Well, we will definitely find some kind of treasure."

Lia looks back at me. "I swear, if we see a snake and you run off screaming..."

"Still?"

She looks back at me with a smile that seizes my heart. "Always."

She's a tornado, tossing shovels and rakes and tomato posts, making all kinds of noise. So I dive in, and we pull out the old boxes, the terracotta planters. We drag out the riding mower and the wheelbarrow. With Lia it's easy to get lost in a job or idea and just follow her.

"I think you should have a yard sale."

She stands up straight. "Hmm, you know, that's not a bad idea." She bites her lip and nods. "That's a really good idea, Matthew."

And with that, the treasure hunt is put on hold, and Lia gets more involved with tearing things out of the garage. But every time I ask her about an item, she stares at it, shakes her head, and declares there is no way she can part with *that*.

Two hours later our "For Sale" pile consists of glass jars, two push mowers, a few gas canisters, and some old window frames. A tiny pile in front of the Honda. The "Absolutely-Not-For-Sale" pile, which is everything else, fills the garage. Somehow it's worse than before we began.

I'm trying to convince Lia to sell a wicker chair when she throws up her hands and declares it's lunch time.

Because she has not yet bothered to go grocery shopping, we take a trip to Crave Sub for lunch. Lia lets me drive, and I jump behind the wheel of the Chrysler, pushing the D button and enjoying the oversized thin steering wheel.

Lia's hair flies in the wind with her wild blouse. I'm a bit worse off, in a ratty t-shirt and camo shorts and smeared in oil and grease from all the machinery I've been moving.

We find a table outside, and she orders the veggie feast and I'm laughing at her because her eyes light up like we're at Time Square. And that's the thing I love most about her, how the most ordinary events turn into something magical.

She's going on about the yard sale and how she wants to make flyers and I'm laughing, reminding her she's only got like, three things to sell, when Mr. Yearly walks up to our table.

He looks at Lia for a few seconds and then eyes me carefully. "Matt, I thought we agreed on you coming back to work today?"

"Oh." I look around, the realization dawning on me that, yes, I did agree to take my job back. But then the game and everything else. "Um, Mr. Yearly, look, I..."

I *what?* I've got nothing. I mean, here I am, greased and sweaty, having lunch with a beautiful girl who is not his granddaughter. Enough said, he squints in the sun. He's still got his apron on and I suppose he's just picking up lunch. He likes to do that on Saturdays. How did I not remember?

"Sorry, Mr. Yearly. I guess I forgot."

He cuts his dusty blue eyes to Lia again. "I reckon you did."

Lia sets down her sandwich. "Well, he did get injured last night. You can't expect him to work all day after suffering a concussion, can you?"

Mr. Yearly opens his mouth to say something to her, then shuts it and nods at me. "No, I suppose not. But...well," he nods toward the door. "I'd better grab lunch."

He shuffles inside, and I'm sure I'm fired all over again. And I should care more, about my commitments and obligations—as my dad would call them—but with Lia's lips curving into a grin, the sun playing with both her hair and her eyes like they were its own personal toys, I can't muster the energy to fulfill them.

Lia cocks her head at me. "I thought you were fired, anyway."

"I was, but then I sort of got my job back." I look to the door where some kids come strolling out. "I think I just got fired again, though."

She nudges me with her foot. "You can work for me, then. Linus isn't pulling his weight with the grass situation."

I laugh. "I'm expensive."

Lia squints at me. "We can work something out." And with that, she pulls out the crumpled script. "Now, help me with my lines."

Sunday afternoon and Dad isn't happy with me. Yes, I suffered a concussion. But no, I am not to "abandon" my responsibilities.

"I won't ask what's going on in your personal life. But I think we both know something has changed. Something big."

"Dad, look. I honestly forgot, okay? I forgot that I was supposed to work. That's the truth."

He doesn't look happy about it. He gets up and heads for the kitchen. Mom pats my knee and asks me for the thousandth time how I'm feeling.

"Mom, I'm fine." I think about Lia in my room. Lunch. Treasure hunting. "It's confusing."

She nods.

Dad comes back with a glass of water. He takes a sip. "I'm trying, Matt. I really am. But what am I supposed to do, let you throw everything away and just run down there and…"

"Dad, look…the football thing. I'm not cleared to play. I guess we'll know more tomorrow."

"But, Matt, either way, playing or not. You need to be there with your team. Supporting your teammates, cheering them on, and helping the underclassmen. You know that. It's all part of the deal. And the job, you're going to have to find something else, because—"

Mom looks up. "Ken, can we just slow down here?"

Dad nods. While he's come a long way, he's still my dad, Mr. Do Right, no matter what. But Mom has always been more of a follow your heart kind of person, and my heart is pulling me down to Lia's house.

That evening I get a call from Coach who tells me I'm most likely going to be out for the next game, but he fully expects me to be at practice. I tell him I will be there. But I might be late.

He grumbles. But I stick to my guns. Tomorrow is Lia's audition, and I'm not missing it. Lia is a friend and I'm committed to supporting her. It's what friends do, they support each other.

And to me that's following both Mom and Dad's advice.

Chapter 23

I should've called Jen. No, not called, but gone to her house and talked to her in person. Instead I was with Lia, cleaning the garage, treasure hunting, out to lunch when we saw Mr. Yearly. Friday seems like a year ago, when I left things scattered everywhere so that one big mess awaits on Monday morning.

Getting out of my car, the first person I see is Tyler. He asks how I'm doing, and I go through the motions, even as he keeps looking me over, up and down until it gets a little awkward. "So, tough night Friday."

I throw my arm through my bookbag strap. "Yeah."

"My ass is still sore from that goat." He laughs.

I guess he's trying to talk about Lia. I look around and don't see the Chrysler so I guess she's not here yet.

Through the parking lot, everyone asks how I'm feeling. Austin asks. James asks. Everyone in passing asks. I'm fine. I'm fine. I'm fine.

I should be grateful, but I just want to talk to Jen. At least until I spot her at her locker with Sarah and Courtney who shoot me their finest scowls. Jen wipes her eyes and keeps her head low. A deep breath, and I make my way over to her.

"Hey, Jen, can we talk?"

All three girls drop their mouths and roll their eyes. Jen shakes her head, pure disdain in her wet glare. Sarah whispers how she cannot believe me. Courtney informs me there's not much to talk about.

I try again. "Maybe later?"

The bell rings. Sarah rolls her eyes. I make my way to class.

School has sort of fallen into its routine by now. Signs are up for the audition and the newness of being back has quickly worn off. The announcements skim over Friday night's loss and stay upbeat and positive that the season is young and we'll bounce back.

I see Lia a few times in the hallways, but I don't rush up to her. It's weird, how it's so much easier when we're at Higgins' place.

By lunch I've had enough of the questions and the glares from Sarah and Courtney. Tyler's not so passive aggressive inquiries about Lia. I don't even go to the cafeteria, where I'm sure they're huddled at the table, glowering and rolling their eyes. Instead, I go outside, where I find her playing disc golf.

I watch as she argues with a kid about where her frisbee landed. She actually stamps her foot and the kid backs off. I laugh for the first time that day.

She turns and sees me and then gets back to her shot. After a few practice motions she tosses the frisbee in the basket, then throws her hands up victoriously. "And still, the champ."

The kid with the swept-over hair throws his head back. "You cheated."

Lia whirls around. "I did no such thing."

"You moved your disc. You always do."

She waves him off and comes walking over to me, basking in her lunch time victory. The three freshmen look at me with a mix of envy and hatred in their eyes. Lia stops a few feet short. "Are you lost?"

"Ha, what? No."

"Oh," she says and then twirls for no other reason but to do it. She nods toward the cafeteria. "Well, I'm not going back in there, so…"

"No, it's…" My stomach growls, because I am hungry. But I'm with Lia, and the last thing I want to do is go in the cafeteria. "So, I was wondering if you needed some last minute prep? Want to go over your lines?"

Her eyes widen. She places her right hand over her heart. "But Stanley, how could you? After everything else, how could you doubt my feelings for you?"

"Um, Rosalina, you...er..." I laugh. "I'm going to need the script."

Lia squeals. She grabs me by the arm and leads me over to the brick wall where she digs in her bookbag, some sort of plaid case thing I'm sure she found in Higgins' house, and produces the rolled and marked script.

She hands it to me. "I know my lines pat, but I want to run some things by you. Particularly page twenty-six, bottom paragraph, where Rosalina finds out Stanley is otherwise involved."

I smile at her. "Otherwise..." I shake my head. "You've uh, put some thought into this."

She throws her hair up on top of her head. Her shirt lifts and I try not to look at her stomach but it's not so easy. She smiles at me. I bury my eyes to the script and find page twenty-six.

The freshmen yell to her, "Hey, Lia, rematch?"

Lia shakes her head at them. "I have to go over my lines."

They nod, deflated as they turn and slink off. She looks at me and pouts. "Poor babies, they're lost without me." She watches them for another second and then turns back to me, her eyes ablaze.

"Stanley. It's been what, seven years?"

I fumble through the words, finding the right spot. Clear my throat. "Eight, to be exact. You look good, my dear."

She narrows her gaze, and if we weren't outside Maycomb High School, the trashcan overflowing with discarded paper plates, milk cartons, pizza crusts, I would swear we were in Europe in the 1950's. "Yes, well, I may look good, but it seems that you have enjoyed the good fortune between us. How's married life?"

Lia paces the dirt path between us, I smile but she does not. She's completely in character and doesn't seem the least bit concerned about the passing stares or attention we're attracting.

"It's fine." The script says I sigh, gaze off wistfully. "Not what I was hoping for, but it's fine."

Lia clicks her teeth. "Hoping for? And what do you suppose you were hoping for? A fairy tale ending? Everlasting love? Hope? You've never been patient, that is certainly clear, had you been..."

"Had I been what? Patient? It's been years! Years have passed!"

Lia shakes her head and whispers, "I was patient."

I look up from the script, where Lia's last line is noticeably absent. She holds my gaze, and I'm caught between this play and her energy. I can't tell if she's acting or if it's something else. I open my mouth to say something, to ask her about the night in my room, when she whips back from Rosalina to Lia and says, "Okay, I think we got it. I have to get to gym."

I nod, scanning the lines again, but I don't see *I was patient*. She takes the script from me, and I blink. "What time is the audition?"

She stuffs the papers in her little plaid bag and picks it up like a brief case. The bright sun hits her eyes, and they flash gold. "Two-thirty, sharp."

"Okay, I told Coach I would be late for practice. Do you mind if I come?"

She stops and smiles. "Of course not."

"Okay."

"Well, thanks for...coming out."

"Yeah. See you onstage."

She turns and walks off, around the school, taking the field and not the hallways as she heads for the gym. The bell rings and the freshmen yell to her, and she playfully shakes her fist at them.

I look back to the cafeteria, and Jen and Sarah are watching me from the window.

Chapter 24

Since everyone is talking about our big loss to Ellison today, I figured play auditions would be a rather low-key affair. But as I arrive at the auditorium lobby I find it packed with drama types. Kids are sprawled out on the floor, on benches, on the steps out front. Others pace and preen while going over their lines with little support groups to help them along the way.

It's like I stumbled upon a new universe. Here, the quiet kids I normally see in passing are prepped and giddy. And while I knew Sarah was big on drama, I wasn't quite prepared to see Jen until I nearly run smack into her.

"Oh, hey," I say, and since she can't ignore me much longer she looks off and grumbles hello. I barrel into my rehearsed apology. "Look, I'm sorry about this weekend. I should've called you."

She turns to me, glowering. "Called. Come by. Not gone to lunch with that slut."

I blink my eyes, stunned by her language. "Um, excuse me?"

"*Tee hee.* My name is Lia and all the little freshmen boys love me." She bounces around and, while she's not going out for the play, she's doing an excellent job of acting. I've never seen this side of her before. She drops the act and glares at me. "Come on. My grandfather gives you a second chance with your job and you don't even bother to show up. Sure, what you did to me was one thing, but..." She shakes her head, at a loss to locate words that describe how truly awful I am.

"Jen, look. I don't want things to be like this between us. But..."

Over her shoulder I spot Lia. She's pacing, talking to herself, which isn't weird because of all the other kids doing the same thing.

Again, this place is full of kids dancing without fear, singing without a care in the world. And it dawns on me: this is exactly where Lia needs to be.

Something else occurs to me a bit too late. That Jen, as she turns and follows my gaze, maybe thought I'd come here to patch things up between us. Now, realizing I'm here to support Lia, she closes her eyes with a sigh. "You know what, Matt. Screw you."

She turns and huffs off. More of this Jen I've never seen. And I hate that I'm the one who brought it out of her. It's not how I want things to end between us. I call out for her but she only throws up her hand.

Across the room, Sarah takes her in with a hug, and it's here, in a lobby full of drama, where she's free to fall into her friend and cry while Sarah tries to turn me to stone with her eyes. I take a breath and look away. Well, senior year is off to a spectacular start.

Courtney joins the party and glowers at me as Jen slumps between her and Sarah on the bench. Not for the first time, I think of what would have been if Lia hadn't shown up out of the blue and found me. Would I be here holding hands with Jen to support Sarah? Would I not have fumbled Friday night? Would we have won the game? Would I be happy, with football and popularity and hanging out every day without the treasure hunts and spur of the moment adventures?

I can't say, but as I trek across the lobby, find Lia, and take a seat sideways, my back against the wall and my knees pulled up on the bench, I'm more than okay with whatever I'm doing now.

Lia paces three steps, talking with her hands, before she sees me and stops. A huge smile blooms on her face. And maybe I'm a jerk—okay yeah, I *know* I'm a jerk—because I should care more that my girlfriend of four months hates my guts, that all her friends hate my guts—but as Lia's feet squeak to a halt and her eyes soak up the afternoon sun and brighten so hopefully, I don't.

I am the happiest jerk you've ever seen.

EVENTUALLY WE'RE CALLED into the auditorium. I wish Lia good luck and find a seat off to the side, about midway up. Only weeks ago I was here to greet incoming freshmen for orientation. Austin and I came out wearing our shiny Maycomb High football jerseys to give some words of wisdom to the terrified faces in the seats.

Three years before that I was here with Mom and Dad, still suntanned and dizzy from my summer with Lia. She'd left by then, and I was heartbroken, but I'd found a confidence I never relinquished. Everyone noticed by the time the school year started, and the growth spurt that followed that year didn't hurt. I was no longer little Matt Crosby, the timid kid who tried to hide in the cracks, but a person who wasn't afraid to stand up for what I believed.

Mrs. Morgan greets the hopefuls, offering a few words of insight and advice. For a woman so short she has no problem throwing her voice clear to the back of the auditorium. It's obvious she's done her share of performing, it's in her every gesture as she explains how casting is subjective. She will do her best to see that everyone finds a role or a part in *Garden Variety*, one of her favorite plays, but notes that there will be many plays and many roles—part of her dizzying production schedule this year. She introduces her assistant and leads the charge of applause because she's so excited.

Auditions for the part of Frank go first. It's a supporting role as I know from my lines with Lia. I watch several guys, ranging in height and looks and stage presence. It gets painful at times, watching kids forget their lines, but nothing dampens Mrs. Morgan's spirits. She's a force of positivity, helping them along and nodding to those doing well.

I can already guess it's down to either Jeremy Fulcher or Alex O'Connell, as they both do well. I slump in my seat as an hour goes by, and it's obvious I'm not going to be late for practice but miss it all together. By the time the part for Rosalina starts, I've shut my phone off because it's buzzing with text messages.

Sarah is good, but I already knew that. She's been at it since preschool with fine arts clubs and summer camps. Her Rosalina is technical, crisp and confident, with just enough emphasis on a woman who has loved and lost and is desperate to find it again. And while her stage presence is palpable, I feel like something is missing. But what do I know?

The next three girls bungle their lines, and Mrs. Morgan says it's no big deal, lines can be memorized. She tells them they're all wonderful.

And then comes Lia.

I sit up in my seat. A certain energy comes over the auditorium. I don't think the lights actually dim or that a spotlight comes down on her, but it almost seems that way. And not just that, I can feel the shifting and glaring coming from Jen and Courtney, probably hoping she'll trip and fall on her face.

Lia has changed into one of the old dresses from Higgins' house. Her hair sits up in a bun that bounces as she strides to the middle of the stage. Without introduction or hesitation she lets it rip, going full tilt Rosalina with a slight accent to her words. Her eyes blaze with intensity as she roars through the monologue, talking with her hands as her entire body demonstrates how the one love she's found was enough for a lifetime. And again, while she's dressed rather conservative in the old dress, the top button is undone and there's something sexy about it.

Whatever she was doing out in the yard at lunch was nothing, child's play. Because right now, I'm watching Rosalina. That much is clear.

At one point, when I manage to take my eyes off Lia so I can peek at Mrs. Morgan, I catch her whispering to her assistant, though her eyes never leave the stage. The assistant nods, smiles, raises her eyebrows, and mouths, "Wow."

Lia finishes and starts off stage when Mrs. Morgan calls after her, almost gushing. "Excuse me?"

Lia stops and turns to them with a smile.

"Well, that was powerful."

Lia nods and thanks them.

Mrs. Morgan consults her notes. "And your name? Lia, correct?"

"Yes. Lia Banks."

Mrs. Morgan nods. Her voice is different, without all the pomp it had earlier. "Lia, that was quite impressive."

Lia blinks and smiles. "Thank you."

Mrs. Morgan only smiles, watching as Lia makes her way offstage. Half an hour later, she thanks everyone for coming and promises to post the cast soon.

I wait for Lia in the lobby, which is a huge mistake because just as soon as I come out and I'm blinking into the bright lobby lights, I overhear Jen and Sarah and Courtney talking about how "over the top" Lia was.

"And what was up with that accent?"

"Or the dress?"

"Or the hair, wow. Try much?"

They see me and stop talking. Their matching glares tell me to get away and stay away. I head for the doors to wait on the steps.

Ten minutes later Lia leap frogs over me and spins around. "So, that was fun." She's changed back to shorts, her hair kind of up but kind of down.

I shake my head. "Hey, Rosalina."

She shoots me a look. "Yeah, I don't know."

I scramble to my feet and we start walking to the parking lot. I pretend not to see people looking at us. The other hopefuls, the parents, the football guys leaving the field. I can hear Coach letting me have it.

Lia pays no attention to any of it. She circles me, does some sort of twirl, and assures me she's fine with any role, even if it's not the lead.

"Okay but, Lia, you know you got that part, right?"

She sets her face to the sun. "I like to keep expectations low. That way I'm always surprised."

"Okay, well, I'm just telling you. The lead is yours."

We get to her car and she stops and takes a big breath. "Well, want to go celebrate?"

I laugh, nudging her foot to mess with her. "What happened to low expectations?"

Austin and the guys start toward us, sweaty from what must have been a grueling practice. Coach isn't nice to us after a win, after a loss it's brutal. From the looks of things they ran a few miles. Austin nods my way.

Lia laughs. "I meant celebrate my audition. The fact I got up there and did it."

For the first time it dawns on me that Lia does feel things like pressure, embarrassment, maybe even shyness. I nod. "Okay, yeah."

She squeals and leaps into her car. "Well, where to?"

"Matt." Austin and Aiden call me over. I guess they want to know where I've been.

Lia pats her seat. "I'm thinking ice cream."

"Yeah, um. Can I meet you there? I have my car and all."

She looks past me, to the football guys. "Oh, yeah sure, okay. But don't take all day, and don't let them make you feel bad for not practicing. Hello? Concussion."

I'm already chuckling. "Okay, I won't."

Lia tears off, the top down and her hair flying.

Austin watches. "So, Preacher Higgins gave her that car?"

I shrug. Aiden nods. "Dude, he gave her his house. My dad said he'd lost his mind, said the church should contest it."

I turn to Aiden. "Contest *what*?"

He looks at me. "The will. That's crazy."

"The church kicked him out. What could they contest?"

Aiden looks at Austin, who's watching Sarah and Jen and Courtney walk out of the auditorium. Great. Aiden laughs. "Well, he did have a gay wedding in his yard. What did he expect?"

I gaze off at Lia at the stoplight, tapping on the steering wheel.

"It's been what, three years since that wedding? The church and everyone else might want to get over it."

Aiden starts to say something but Austin gives me a playful shove. "So uh, how's your head? Thought you were coming to practice."

"Yeah, well. I missed it. Not much I can do anyway."

"So is that it, you're going to quit?"

"I didn't say that. I just, I'm not cleared to play on Friday."

"Lucky you. We did five miles."

"That sucks."

Lia pulls off. I grab my keys. "Well, I gotta run."

Austin and Aiden exchange looks. Aiden nods toward the road where Lia's driving off. "Yeah, I bet. So, you and Jen done?"

I open my mouth to say something, but why? I let it go. "Well, we need to talk, but I think so, to be honest."

Austin nods. He looks back at Sarah and Jen, now watching us. I look at Austin, then follow his gaze toward Jen, and I wonder how long that's been brewing. Maybe I should care, but I don't. I can't. I toss my keys up and catch them.

"Well, see you tomorrow."

Chapter 25

After stuffing ourselves with ice cream, Lia and I search the basement. Maybe not so much search as Lia has me move everything—shelves, boxes, old appliances, a cast iron woodstove—from one end of the basement to the other hoping to find clues. When I ask about the riddles she waves me off.

"You don't understand how Higgins' mind worked."

"And you do," I mutter. She shushes me and we sift through more and more relics from the past. More gambling receipts, more sketches, more paintings, and more sides to Higgins than I'd ever guessed. Painter, high roller, poet, it never ends with this guy.

All we end up doing is making more of a mess. Just like the garage. It's nearly ten when we give up and head upstairs. I tell Lia for the hundredth time how well she did at auditions.

She pulls out the dog tag from her shirt. "I think my dad would be happy about it."

I remember her telling me how she and her dad used to watch old cinema together, it's where she got her flare for the dramatic, so to speak.

I smile at her and nod. "I'm sure he would be, and not just because of the auditions."

She looks to me and smiles. Our eyes lock for a few seconds before she brushes away from me. "Such a charmer, Matthew."

I laugh. "What's that supposed to mean?"

Lia strolls into the kitchen and shrugs her shoulders. "At school. It's something to see. Three years ago you were scared of your own shadow, and now...well..."

I follow her to the table, still covered with more notes and gambling cards.

And where the pines stand, and the buzzards roost, the golden sun shall set and lead the way.

And it's here, or near, or down below, where the rock and the tree grow together.

The rock and the tree. Gibberish. I glance at Lia. "Well, wasn't it you who told me to be more confident?"

She looks up at me, her lips part but she doesn't say anything, only nods.

I want to ask if she's going to stay this time or disappear like she did three years ago. But she gets up suddenly and opens the fridge. "I really need to get to the grocery store."

"Now?"

She nods. I think about homework. Jen. The play. Football practice. Mom and Dad.

"Well, want some company?"

Mom and I arrive at Doctor Stinnett's office the next afternoon. She wants to be absolutely sure I'm cleared to play before I set foot on the field. Even after I spent the weekend "treasure hunting" with Lia, digging holes, finding rocks, roots, and one rusted horse shoe Lia was so excited about she kissed me.

At the office, I fill out the clipboard worksheets and answer as honestly as I can. Headaches that won't go away. No. Vomiting. No. Unusual behavior. Hmm.

Dr. Stinnett is about Mom's age, with short dark hair and glasses. She invites me in and looks me over. She checks my pupils and asks about the symptoms.

She goes over the long term effects of concussions, about

returning too early. She asks how I'm doing, what I've been feeling. I tell her I've been confused, not since the concussion, but before even. When I fumble over my words she tells me it's fine and we go through all the tests and procedures. She talks about the brain as though it were a computer. Her face is open and concerned and it feels like she's expecting me to beg her to let me return to the field.

"I know how hard this must be for you."

I nod.

She sits down, checks her computer, and then looks me in the eye. "I'd say in the meantime you can return to practice, but no contact." She gets my attention. "Got it?"

I glance around the room. At the painting of a field and a barn. I think about Higgins and his artwork on display. I had no idea the guy could paint. That he was gambling on horses. That he had a life outside of Maycomb, it seems.

"Matt?"

"Yes? Sorry."

She looks at me. "How do you feel about this?"

"Well," I take a breath. "I'm willing to follow your advice. I don't want to return to the field too early, so if you're of the opinion I should sit, I'll sit."

She tilts her head, brow furrowing. I realize I may have poured it on a bit too thick.

"Really?"

I nod.

She eyes me carefully before turning away, but suddenly she seems more relaxed. "You must be the first football player I've had in here for a concussion who isn't crying, cursing, or groaning about a second opinion."

I shrug. "I just...I don't know. Honestly, I don't really want to play right now."

"Oh," she glances up from the computer. I picture her listing this as some sort of behavioral change. Another symptom.

I shift, the paper on the exam table crinkling too loud. "No, I just mean…there's been a lot of changes in my life recently and…"

I turn back to the painting, the field, the grass, thinking about the pond, wondering what I'm doing, talking to this doctor like she's a counselor or something. I laugh, kick my feet from the bench. "I guess, I'm not having any symptoms, no dark thoughts or anything like that. It's hard to explain."

She nods and smiles to put me at ease. "It's completely understandable. How about I hold off on clearing you for practice or anything for now? We can rethink this when you're ready."

I can't help the smile that comes across my face. "Okay, yeah."

Of course Mom freaks out. Being not cleared to play leads her to think I'm severely damaged. She calls Dad, armed with a fact sheet about concussions, and we sit in the parking lot as he goes in and out on the speaker, talking about second opinions until Mom shuts him down.

She gets off the phone and looks over at me, studying me for signs of trauma or permanent damage. I quickly look away and debate whether to tell her the truth.

But what is the truth?

"Matt, I just…are you being honest with me?"

I turn to her, wondering if she actually read my mind.

She looks to the sheet and frowns. "You haven't gotten sick, right? Are you sleeping okay, and your thoughts, you're not having…"

I shake my head. "Mom. No. None of that, really, I promise."

She stares at me, looking for signs.

I sigh. "Mom, I don't want you to tell Dad this, but, I don't really want to play football right now. And I know about the scholarships and everything but…" I look to the window again. "He'll just blame it on Lia."

Mom sets the sheet aside. "I see. Well, I'm completely okay with you not playing football. I was against it in the first place." She starts the car. "All your dad needs to know is that you aren't cleared to play."

"And Coach?"

She puts the car in gear. "If your coach doesn't like it, he can deal with me."

I FIND Coach Cutright before school the next day. He's in his classroom, where he teaches health in the afternoons.

He looks up from a notebook and smiles. "Matt, how you feeling?"

"I'm good," I say, the truth. I haven't had any headaches or nausea or anything else I was told to be aware of. In fact, I feel like I could play. Even though I can't.

"That's good. Missed you yesterday."

His way of saying "where were you?"

Again, Maycomb's glory days were back when my dad played. They fell on hard times after that, probably because most of the bigger city schools were more crowded. Coach Cutright arrived four or five years ago and turned things around in a hurry. And he did it by recruiting. I'll never forget him finding me in gym class at the beginning of last year, after my second growth spurt, asking me to come out for the team.

Dad was thrilled, beyond thrilled when Coach put me in at tight end, where I had enough speed to get open and enough size to block a linebacker. A natural fit, they liked to call it. I just never loved it the way my teammates do. The way my dad did.

Coach flips through the notebook on his desk. "So protocol has you out this week, but that doesn't mean you're not a part of this team," he says, echoing my dad. Then he looks at me directly. "I need you out there, going through plays and scouting. And we got that early bye week so that helps. Get ready for Hanford."

Hanford. I remember Dad poring over the schedule. He's already worked it out with the jail to have off on Friday nights, then

Saturdays when we make the playoffs. It's all assumed this year. This is the year. This *was* the year.

I tell myself to say it. To tell Coach to his face I don't want to play anymore. To quit. To quit on my team and my commitments. Instead, I study the floor tiles.

Coach lowers his head. "Something on your mind?"

"Well, uh, I may be out this week though. I'm helping out with theater and..."

Coach laughs. "Matt. Look. It's okay to be afraid. You took a hell of a shot. But you gotta put it behind you, hear?"

I nod.

He sits back in his chair, setting out his massive chest. "You took a lick and you're okay. This is all just procedure. Back in my day, in your old man's day, we would've sat out a play, dusted ourselves off, and run back out there ready to give it back to somebody. But now we got rules, it leaves you off the field, to think. To think too much."

I let out a sigh. "Yeah, thing is, right now I need to help a friend, that's all."

"Heard something about that."

The bell rings. Coach looks to the door. "Look, don't let some girl ruin this for you, okay? Seen it too many times."

I jerk my head up to him, then look back to the door. *Is this guy serious?* I fix my bookbag on my shoulder. "Well, I gotta get to class."

He nods, gets back to his desk. "Listen, Matt. I'll see you this afternoon."

"Yeah."

Lia and I eat lunch outside. Her freshmen groupies shoot me dirty looks. I picture them jumping me in the parking lot for taking their beautiful leader from them.

Lia's got her head buried in her notes. Since the audition she hasn't said much about it, though I can tell it's driving her crazy. Casting doesn't go up until Friday afternoon.

"I think we try the pond again. He loved the pond."

I tear into my slice of pizza. "You think he buried the treasure in the pond?"

She rolls her eyes. "Maybe. He could've."

I sit back. "Lia, what if there, um, is no treasure?"

She slaps my arm. "You can't give up so easily. Besides, if there is no treasure, well, at least we are having fun."

"So we drain the pond. What about your ducks?"

"We're not draining the pond, okay?"

"Scuba diving?"

"You're impossible."

That much is true. I have an impossible smile on my face. Because I'm sitting at lunch, outside in the warm sun with Lia. At school. It's all impossible.

She gets back to her notes. I just smile. The freshmen glare at me, and somewhere inside the cafeteria, people are probably talking about how I've lost my mind.

Let them talk. I don't care.

But my dad cares. When I get home from school he's in the living room, waiting. Never good.

"Matt. Hey, how you feeling?"

"I'm feeling sick of that question."

Dad nods. "Yeah, I bet. So, I heard about the doctor visit. That's tough."

I search his face, wondering what he knows, if he means it. Maybe Coach called him, told him to light a fire under my ass or whatever he would've said.

I shrug. Mom must still be at work so I have no back up in my corner. Before I can come up with an answer, Dad wipes his chin and crosses his legs. "Matt, look, a lot has happened the past few weeks. And I know you can't play this week, but that doesn't mean..."

"I know. I know. I'm still part of a team and need to support my teammates. Dad." I turn to the window. I don't know how to say it. "I don't really want to play football. It was never really my thing to begin with and..."

Dad sits up, suddenly interested. Almost panicked. "Don't want to play? What do you mean it's not your thing? Matt, you're a preseason all-conference honorable mention."

He sighs. "Look. We've been down this road before. I get it, she's back and you're confused. But look, you're not fourteen, I'm not going to tell you what to do, okay? But up until she came back you were fine, you had a plan and everything was worked out."

"Dad, I'm not confused though. And plans change. My grades haven't slipped and I...I don't know. I'm not saying that I'm quitting the team, at least I don't think I am. I just, yeah, up until she came back I was okay with going through the motions. But I never felt like it was me, does that make sense?"

It doesn't make sense to Dad, but he's trying, I can see that much. He's come around a lot in the past few years. Since Lia came around the first time.

He gets to his feet, joins me at the window where we gaze out at our yard, the street, at nothing. "Look, this is your decision. I won't tell you what to do. But I do feel like if you are cleared to play, you have an obligation to fulfill."

I nod. "Okay. Thanks for listening, Dad."

He smiles. The mood lightens. Dad squeezes my shoulder. "How's the Chrysler holding up?"

I laugh. "Dad, Lia will let you drive it, you know."

He turns to me, his eyes wide as a kid's. "You think so?"

Chapter 26

I skip practice again. I know it's wrong, but Lia won't let up about her "hunch" with the treasure, and so I follow her down to the pond, where her ducks sit in the corner, watching us dig a hole near the gigantic sycamore tree.

Correction, I dig, Lia paces, going over her lines even as I promise her she already got the part. I jam the shovel in the dirt and hit yet another root.

"Well, if I got the part, as you say, I'd better know these lines backward and forward, right?"

"You might get Rosalina's understudy," I say just to mess with her.

She glares at me for a second, then shrugs. "That's fine, too."

I wipe the sweat from my forehead. "So, how do you like Maycomb High, so far?"

She smiles, reaches over and wipes my forehead, looks at her hand then wipes her palm on my shirt. "It's okay. Very, clique-ish. And what are there, six black kids? Well, seven now, now, I guess."

I'd never thought of it that way. But she's right, it is clique-ish. "Yeah, you seem to be carving out your own little group though."

She smiles. "My freshmen?"

"Yeah." I get around the root. "So, what are we looking for? Gold? Silver?"

She shrugs, walks off and twirls like she did when she was fourteen. She spins around and catches me watching her. "Who knows, right?"

I laugh. She tells me to take a break and we sit on the dock. And she's naming the ducks when I remember something. I peek over and see it's still there, carved into a plank. I nudge her with my elbow.

M&L

Her eyes light up with her smile. "When did you do that?"

I shrug. "Right before you left. When I was down here by myself one day."

She stares at it, pouting some. "I'm sorry I didn't say goodbye. It was just, too hard, you know?"

I nod, remembering how hard it was to find out she was gone, after I'd looked around for her, hoping maybe it was one of her more elaborate pranks. It was Mr. Higgins who finally told me. He was the one who gave me her father's dog tag.

Lia's hand slides over mine. She sets her head on my shoulder and there's nothing else to say. She left. She's back. I hope she'll stay.

The ducks flutter their wings. Lia's head pops up and she nudges me with her shoulder. "Hey, back to work for you."

We spend the next hour digging, hitting more roots, finding more rocks. Lia lets me off the hook around eight, and we start back for the house.

I'm sweaty and filthy. She offers to hose me off. We're laughing so hard about it we don't even notice the shiny red Jeep in the driveway, or the figure leaning against it, until we almost walk right into him.

"Oh." Lia looks up suddenly. "Hi, Tyler."

"Hi, Lia." Tyler looks at me. "Hey, Matt."

We stand there for a minute, until it gets weird. Tyler's all put together, bright and clean. He smells like he's been swimming in a vat of body wash. Lia sneezes.

"So, um, Lia, I was just dropping by." He looks at me again. "To say hey, maybe try to make friends with your goat, if that's okay?"

Lia shoots him a look. "Are you sure?"

"Well, I feel bad for running off like that and all." Tyler grins, throws a glance my way. I can tell he's the sort of guy who doesn't like to lose or look bad. But after what he said about Lia, I'm all set to escort him off the premises.

Lia giggles. "How's your...?" She gestures to her backside. "You know?"

Tyler looks around, blushing some. "Oh, it's, I'm okay."

Gesturing toward the back, Lia gives him one last chance to back out. "If you're sure? Okay, he's back here. I'll let you feed him."

She runs inside, leaving me with Tyler and all the awkwardness he's brought with him.

"So, uh, what's up with the shovel?"

"Oh." I look at it like I have no idea where it came from. "We were um, planting some stuff," I nod to the woods, "back there."

"Oh. Hey, man, I didn't know you were here, didn't know you were—"

Lia comes busting out. "Okay, I found some carrots. If this doesn't get you on his good side there's simply no hope for you."

We troop around the house, Tyler and me following Lia. I'm trying to play nice but wondering what's going on—obviously Tyler is still trying with Lia. Sure enough, we find Linus on top of his little house in his pen. His water bowl thrown to the side and he's done some damage to the fencing.

Lia shakes her head. "I hate leaving him in here, but he runs off." She bends down, baby talking to the goat. "Don't you? You just run right off."

She stands, motions to Tyler, and hands him the carrots. It's obvious he has no desire to feed the goat, and it takes him a minute as he's too busy staring at Lia's legs.

"Okay, so you should be good," Lia urges.

"Thanks." Linus starts ramming the cage, and Tyler jumps back.

Lia's laugh echoes off the back of the house. "Whoa. He really does *not* like you." She turns to the goat. "Now Linus, that is no way to treat a guest."

Good boy, Linus. I lean on the shovel with a smile, happy to watch as Tyler eases closer, pinching the carrot by the green so it dangles and Linus has to snap his jaw several times to get it. When he does, Tyler leaps back. I duck my head in my arm and laugh.

Tyler tries once again, but it's the same result.

Finally, Lia shoves him out of the way. "Oh, for goodness sake." She starts feeding Linus.

Tyler glances at me and I frown. He looks to Lia again. "So, I heard you did really well at auditions. Think you got the lead?"

She stands up and bites her lip. I hold my breath. She really is something and she has to know it. She has to know she's knocking two guys back at once.

"Ha, well, I don't know. Where did you hear that?"

"Oh, my mom is friends with Mrs. Morgan."

I stand up a bit straighter.

Lia does too. "Really?"

"Yeah, she said you were amazing. Like, she was going on and on about it."

Lia looks at me and smiles. "Well, that's good news, right?"

"I don't think Sarah will be happy, but..."

I nod.

Tyler looks back at me. Then to Lia. "Yeah, I was wondering if you wanted to grab a bite to eat, to celebrate. That is, if..." he looks back at me. "If you aren't busy? And, Matt, maybe you could call Jen?"

The shovel keeps me from falling over. I grip the handle, trying to come up with something to say when Lia looks back to Linus, begging for more carrots. "Ah, thanks for the offer, but I can't celebrate hearsay, you know? I'd rather wait until tomorrow. Make it official."

Tyler nods. "Oh, okay cool. Well, maybe once it's official, then?"

Lia sighs as though she's suddenly bored. "I don't know, Tyler."

Tyler finally takes the hint. "Okay, I gotta run. I'll talk to ya'll tomorrow."

"Yeah, thanks for stopping by."

He nods. "Yeah." He looks at me, and I stare him down. He leaves without saying anything else.

Out front, we hear his Jeep start up. Tyler backing out of the driveway. Lia, back to feeding Linus, looks at me and narrows her eyes with a smirk.

I feign innocence. "What?" Lia keeps a level stare on me, but the smirk is breaking through. "Why are you smiling?"

"Why are *you* smiling?"

"I'm not, am I?"

Lia nods. "Yeah, you are. Big time."

"Oh."

"You know," she says, letting the door to the pen swing open. Linus gallops out and toward me. I scratch his chin. Lia walks over and kneels beside me. "If Linus doesn't trust that boy, neither do I."

"Good boy, Linus."

Chapter 27

I arrive at school early on Friday, where the only sound in the halls is the murmur of study groups from the classrooms. I get to the library and catch up on homework. I'm tired and sore, as Lia had me digging holes all over the five acres of woods behind Preacher Higgins' house. But it's a good kind of sore, like a reminder of our time together.

Today promises to be a weird one. Jen is no longer talking to me, and it's safe to say we have officially broken up. Lia likes to hold my hand, hug me, throw her head against my chest, but it goes no further than that.

It's weird, how I'm in no hurry to get back on the football field. Mom is okay with it, but she wants me to make the right decisions. She wants me to do things the right way. She says Coach deserves to hear it from me. Same goes for Jen.

I looked up at her when she mentioned Jen. She laughed. Said I might as well be screaming my feelings for Lia to anyone near enough. And then I told my mother what I was most afraid of. What if Lia doesn't feel the same way?

Mom said I can't control that. I can only do my part. And that begins with honesty. To myself as well as everyone around me.

So it's a day for honesty. I have to talk to Coach again. I have to talk to Jen and try my best to smooth things over. I promised Mom I would do both of those things. Now I'm in the library, avoiding the parking lot.

I catch up with Jen between third and fourth periods. When she sees me she basically starts speed walking the other way. I rush to catch up to her. "Jen, hey, wait up."

She keeps walking. I get up with her and match her strides. "Jen, please. Can we talk for a sec?"

She stops. "You want to talk? Now? Between classes?"

"Well, I..." Hmm, she's got a point. "Look I just wanted to see how you were doing. And apologize."

She looks at me, searches my eyes as though reading a riddle she doesn't understand. Then she laughs. "Matt, this is just about you feeling better about yourself for breaking up with me, isn't it?"

"No, I, I don't want things to be so..."

"Poor, Matt. Never can have anyone angry at him. Well you know what? You don't get to do that. You don't get to maybe sort of cheat on me, embarrass me, then simply say sorry and we become great friends, okay? So I'll say this one more time. Screw you, Matt."

And then she storms off. Some kids watch, laugh, enjoy the show, but I don't chase after her. I won't anymore. Because if nothing else, she's right. It's not fair for me to expect her to be fine with it.

I turn the other way. Someone slaps me on the back. Calls her crazy. But Jen isn't crazy. She's smart and pretty and talented. And most of all, she's right.

LIA IS a mess of nerves at lunch. Chewing her fingernails and pacing. The freshmen watch closely, shouting extra loud about disc golf in hopes she'll join in.

"I think your fans are calling."

She gnaws on her thumbnail, glances at them. "I don't even care if I get the lead. I just want a part, any part."

I close my eyes and laugh. She slaps my leg. I stare at her until she looks at me. "Is that what you're worried about? Lia, you definitely have a part in that play. Everyone present in the auditorium during auditions knows that."

She keeps on with the nail. One of the little freshmen throws a frisbee that lands a few feet away.

I laugh. "They're getting desperate."

Lia hops up, grabs the frisbee, and slings it toward the net. It curves, keeps curving, and hits a tree near the shop. Her shoulders slump. "See, I can't even do that."

She plops down. I'm about to say something about the casting when she drops her hands in her lap and looks at me. "My mom called last night."

My entire body reacts to the words. A jolt of cold energy rolls down my neck and through my arms. "Oh. Is she, is she out?"

Lia shakes her head, picks at some grass. "No, but... Well, there's always bail."

So many questions. What does this mean? Is Lia leaving again? Would her mom come live with her? But I can't speak, and we sit for another minute, school becoming a distant backdrop to our thoughts.

Lia turns her face to the sky, as though letting the late morning sunshine rinse her clean. Then she looks at me. "She needs money. For said bail."

No. No. No. I sigh. "Lia."

She drops her head, letting her hair fall over her face as she picks at the grass. "I know what you're going to say, okay?" Her is voice sharp and short. Gone are the little accents and gestures, all the smiles and shine. She's talking to me like an adult. She picks a stalk of grass, holds it up, and watches it fly off in the breeze. "You're going to tell me not to give her money. That I can't trust her. You're going to say that she's done this time after time after time and it never works. You're going...oh, you're going to..." She reaches out and collapses into me, a ball of tears and sobs.

And while I'm aware of the people watching, I don't let her go. Not when she slaps my chest, sobbing and yelling into me. I absorb some of what she's feeling, what she's been carrying for too long. I hold her as the freshmen watch, frisbees dangling at their sides, and when a group at the picnic tables points and whispers. I wrap her up tighter and hold on.

"She's never going to stop, ever. And now she's making me feel like crap. She said I was selfish. *I* was selfish, after she's robbed me of everything."

"I'm so sorry, Lia." It's all I can say, when I want to say *don't let her do this to you. Please don't leave me again.* But I don't have a chance to say it, not when a teacher, an assistant coach I recognize, walks over to us.

"Everything all right over here?"

Lia pulls her face away from me, leaves one arm around my neck, and wipes her eyes with her free hand.

I nod. "Yeah, we're fine."

The teacher looks us over, her furrowed brow softening when she sees Lia. Her voice changes, lower now. "Are you sure?"

Lia nods. "Yes, just, something personal."

The teacher nods, looks around. "Okay, well." She looks at me. "You know the rules, I can walk you to guidance if you'd like, but this sort of contact is prohibited."

Lia, her eyes still wet, looks at me and laughs. "Okay, I understand. I mean, I don't really, but... Sorry."

The teacher frowns, aware of how everyone in the courtyard is now watching. "Very well, it's just," again she looks at me. "You know there's a zero tolerance policy, so..." With that she's off.

Lia's glossy eyes go big. "Zero tolerance? Contact? What, like no hugs?"

I lift my shoulders. "I didn't know they were still doing that."

"That's outrageous."

"I agree."

I watch her take in this new information. "Are you serious? No hugging?" She's on her feet now. "What about that tree?" She points to a large oak tree. "Can I hug that tree?"

Here we go. "I think so."

Lia looks around. Tapping her chin. "We should fight this."

"Lia." I take a step toward her. Her eyes are red rimmed, still wet. "Don't we have other things to worry about?"

She shakes her head. The bell rings. "I'm not through with this. I don't want to live in a world where hugs are banned."

So, it's going to be like that. She's going to shut down and refuse to talk about her mom, the pain she's feeling. Okay. I nod. "Yeah."

The rest of the day I think about Lia and her mom. I picture her grabbing her bookbag and walking out of class. Getting in the Chrysler and leaving.

She wouldn't leave, not with the play and the house and Linus, right?

But it's Lia, and there are no rules, no norms to follow, only her heart.

By the final bell I'm ready to sprint to the auditorium, even as my steps instinctively turn toward the gym, to the locker room, to dress out for football practice. I still need to talk to Coach. But the casting, I have to find out.

I turn back and hurry for the auditorium. A few of my teammates ask where I'm headed, looking at me like I'm crazy. But Austin is in the lobby, which is strange, but whatever. I nod and mumble and keep going until I find Lia outside the doors, standing on the padded benches, craning her neck. When she sees me she waves and rushes up to me.

I throw my hands out. "Well?"

She shakes her head. "Well what?"

I roll my eyes. "Did you get the part?"

She looks away, smiling, then takes a step forward and shoves me. "I was waiting for you! Now come on."

We brave the huddles in the lobby. A few kids I remember from auditions are at the board, checking for their names. One girl leaps in place. "Yes."

When they see us, they part. Things go quiet. It's tense, and I feel every eyeball on us. Lia takes a deep breath, peeks at me one last time, and nods. I follow her finger to the list, posted on a makeshift corkboard on an easel. It's not hard to find what we're looking for. Just under Frank.

Rosalina–Lia Banks

My mouth drops, even as I already knew it had to be. Lia stares at the list, the crowd closing in on us. I look at her, waiting for some sort of reaction, but she's only looking at the list, one hand on the dog tag. She glances at me, then back to her name.

"Lia, you did it."

A huge smile spreads across her face. The cast members break into applause. Some pats on the back as Lia, her gaze never leaving mine, takes a running start and leaps into me, her arms and legs wrapping around me as we shatter the no-hug policy into pieces. I swing her around, breathe her in, as her lips brush my ear and she whispers, "I can't believe it."

I think about her at lunch, her mom and jail and how Lia sees herself. "Believe it, you're amazing."

She climbs off me, fixing her hair and beaming that megawatt smile. She gets a few more high fives and congratulates the others, when the door swings open and Sarah and Jen walk into the lobby.

By now, it's sort of obvious to anyone in the room that Lia owns the lead. Sarah looks at Jen, and I can tell they're thinking of turning back but instead come forward. And that's when Austin walks over to Jen, and she gives him a small smile, confirming my suspicions. So that answers that.

I steal a quick glance at the list and spot Sarah's name beside the part for Elizabeth. While it's a big part, wife of Stanley, it's not going to be big enough for her.

Sarah wants the lead. And even as it's sort of obvious by the casts' reaction, they plod forward to see for themselves. Lia smiles at them. Austin sort of stiffens as he looks my way, to gauge my reaction. Jen rolls her eyes and gives me a death stare.

Sarah walks up to the list. She takes a long, lingering gander at it then turns to Jen. "Well, isn't that fitting?"

Jen shakes her head.

Austin nods to me, his way of trying to make things less awkward. "See you at practice, Matty."

They make their way out. Sarah, Courtney, Jen, and Austin, my old supporting cast.

To celebrate, Lia joins Mom and me for dinner. Mom is thrilled with Lia getting the part, and she and Lia talk theater for nearly an hour before we sit down to eat.

My mom has always been enchanted with Lia. Her eyes shine just looking at her, her mouth is always parted with a little smile like when she's watching some old romantic movie.

Lia's going on about her lines, how she's going to use me to practice. What I don't mention is the kissing scene with Stanley—a part that went to Declan Fletcher, a junior of all things. I don't know him well, but I've seen him. He's got long hair and wears old sweaters and corduroy pants and a hemp necklace. Did I mention there's a kissing scene?

Lia gushes about the play. It's not a big play, so there isn't much time until opening weekend. Apparently Mrs. Morgan likes to do many small plays instead of a few big productions. Either way, Lia's nervous and excited and ready to learn everything there is to know about theater, while I keep thinking about the call from her mother and what's going to happen there.

After dinner we walk down to her house. Lia takes my hand and swings it, still going on about wardrobe and everything else *Garden Variety*. We're at her driveway when I finally ask what's been on my mind.

"So Lia, what are you going to do? About your mom?"

She lets go of my hand, and her fingers fly to the dog tag on her chest. She looks off to the woods. "You really wore this the whole time?"

I feel the warmth on my cheeks and look away. "Nah, I just put it on really quick when you came back."

She shoves me. "Stop it."

I take a step closer to her. "Well, I had to take it off when I had surgery."

Her gaze drops to my chest. She reaches up and sets her hand there. "Did it hurt?"

I nod. "Yeah, it did, actually." I think back to the metal rod in my chest for a year. The visits, the tests, the everything. "But I'm a fast healer."

She looks at me, smiling. "I'm glad you did it, if it's what you wanted. Gosh, you've changed so much."

I shake my head, grabbing her hand. "But not really."

She shakes the hair from her face. "You're right. Even though you didn't like the way you looked, it shaped who you are, who you became."

"That's deep, Lia."

She doesn't laugh. "Thank you, Matthew."

I pull my head back. "For what?"

She shrugs. "For…I don't know, for…"

She leans forward and sets her lips to mine. I kiss her back and pull her closer, but before I get lost in my mind she pulls away and smiles. "Come on."

And then she's gone, running down the path, for the pond. And I'm chasing after her, through the trees and the brush and the heat and the haze of memories that haunt the woods around us. We get to the pond and she leaps to the dock. I tell myself it's fine that she doesn't want to talk about her mom right now. It's fine if she had a roller coaster of a day, from the crying to the laughing to the exhilarating reward of the leading role in the play. Lia, who's been in Maycomb for a month and has already altered my path, my life, my future, and whatever memories I'll take with me.

She turns and beckons me toward the water. I climb the dock and we watch the ducks. And she kisses me again. And again. And it's fine. All of it.

It has to be.

Chapter 28

"You come to practice or you're off this team."

Coach's face is an extra shade of maroon. He's fuming, about the opening loss, about the news that I'm sidelined for at least two weeks. I knew he would say something about practice, but it doesn't mean I'm prepared for him to flip out like this. "You're throwing a scholarship away, Matt."

I nod to the paperwork on his desk. "I'm not cleared, Coach. Not much I can do about that."

He shakes his head. I'd never thought of Coach Cutright, great savior of Maycomb High football, to be petulant. It's almost comical, his temper. His eyes flick to the desk then they're back on me. "I would get a second opinion. The guys need you, Matt. It's like you don't want to be on this team. Is that it?"

"I'd rather not have permanent brain damage, if that's what you're asking?"

He glances at the clock. "Practice is at three-fifteen. If you're not there I'll assume you've quit."

I get to my feet. "Thanks, Coach."

He doesn't look up from his desk. I let myself out.

At lunch, we're flipping through the script when I bring up the kiss. Well, not our kiss, but Rosalina's kiss.

Lia looks at me with a smile. "Matthew."

"Lia?"

"As you know, I'm awfully familiar with this script. And there's only one scene with a kiss, and it's rather innocent, at least that's my interpretation. Can you at least try to contain your jealousy?"

I roll my eyes. Her first rehearsal is today, and I don't plan on missing it. This isn't a big play and they won't have long. I look over at her. Then, with a smile, I look at her again. "You'll need to rehearse it though, right?"

Her lips part. She tilts her head. "Yes, at home, many times. In fact, maybe I should call Tyler."

"Ouch."

Austin finds me before practice. "Hey, Matt."

I nod to him and he walks over, strutting with that football swagger. I know the team is looking to get back on track Friday, with Riverside, a notoriously terrible team out of Danville.

"Hey, what's going on, man? How's the noggin?"

I smile. "Ah, I'm okay. Didn't get cleared to play though."

"Yeah, I heard. So, look man, you coming to practice? Eric is struggling."

Eric, the sophomore tight end. He's a big kid, but with heavy feet and hands like bricks. I laugh. "Yeah, I'm uh, I've got something today so..."

Austin drops the act, he scowls at me as a few people pass. "Are you quitting on us, man? This is crazy, first you ditch us at lunch, and the thing with Jen, which, I sort of need to talk to you about, when it's cool and all."

I hold up a hand to cut him off. "Look, Austin. The thing with Jen. If she's fine with it, I'm fine too, you know?"

"Yeah? Okay, I just, to be honest with you I've liked her for a while."

I nod. "Yeah, it's cool, really. I appreciate it. But you don't need my permission or whatever. She can make her own decisions. And with football. I don't know right now, okay?"

He looks down. I can tell it's not what he wants to hear. "Dude, we went through a lot last year, and now it's like you're just walking away."

I can't do this with him, not right now, parroting Coach. "Hey, man, I appreciate your concern." I hook a thumb over my shoulder. "I gotta run, though. Okay?"

"Yeah, okay."

I turn away, feeling his glare on my back. I realize, somewhere in the back of my head, I'm turning on everyone I've known for the past three years. But how did I know this would happen, that Lia would come back and wreck me? I reach for the dog tag that isn't there. Of course it isn't, it's sitting against her chest.

I slide into a seat in the back of the auditorium. It isn't as dark as I'd hoped, but with Jen at soccer practice and the excitement of auditions over, it's easy to slip in, sit, and hopefully go unnoticed.

Mrs. Morgan talks to the cast as a group, maybe fifteen of them, with the set crew lingering, looking at their phones. She talks about commitment until it almost feels like one of Coach's speeches, then her eyes come alive as she speaks of the show and the buzz of performing. Lia's face lights up, and I can't help my smile.

She's got a notebook out, the little nerd, jotting down Mrs. Morgan's instructions, what to expect and all of that, and then they break into groups.

Declan Fletcher saunters over and introduces himself. He's short, about Lia's height, and she smiles and they go over things together. Mrs. Morgan works with the staff and they don't do much else, really.

I let myself out.

That evening, Lia has me dig behind the garage. I ask her if she wants me to rent a bulldozer, and she tells me to shush. She reads her lines, out loud, so that after an hour, I've not only dug three holes, but I've also memorized most of the opening act.

At some point I set both hands on the end of the shovel and try to be casual about it. "So, have you heard anything else from your mom?"

She sets the script down, shakes her head. "No. Well, yes. She left a message."

"Oh." I wait for her to decide how much she wants to talk.

Linus is making a racket in his pen. Lia gazes off to the woods. "You know, bail and all."

"Yeah. And?"

She turns to me. "And what? I'm not doing it. She's taken enough from me—money, time, love, experiences. I'm done."

She sets off into the woods. I plunge the shovel into the ground and keep digging.

Lia lets me off the hook twenty minutes later. "I don't think it's here."

I laugh. "Here as in *here*?" I stab the dirt with the shovel. "Or here as in," I wave my arms, gesture to the woods. "*Here*?"

She nods to the hole. "Here. Or there. But it was good practice, right?"

I toss the shovel down and take a seat next to her, against a tree. "That's what I'm doing, practicing?"

"And helping me with my lines."

I wipe my forehead and move in closer. She shoots me a smile. "I'm not at the kissing scene yet."

"But we could, um, practice."

Lia looks me in the eye as she leans closer. Her eyes search mine, then go higher. "You have dirt on your forehead."

"Oh." I reach for my forehead and Lia jumps up and takes off. I call after her. "Hey."

"Come on, Linus got out."

"Great."

Chapter 29

The hunt for Higgins' treasure isn't all for nothing. While I doubt any treasure exists it's too much fun searching for it with Lia to stop. I go to play rehearsals all week and another doctor visit, while Coach, along with most of the team, continues not to speak to me. But on Friday they beat Riverside and seem to be back on track. I catch Jen in the hall with Austin. They look cozy. And for the first time in weeks she doesn't snarl at me.

Saturday Dad, of all people, suggests we have Lia over for dinner. She arrives around six wearing a thin flannel button down and her customary cutoff jeans. Dad grills burgers, Mom and Lia and I talk about the play. Lia will talk for hours about the play.

We sit down, and Dad brings in a plate of burgers. He gives Lia a hard time about being a vegetarian, but something's off. Sure enough, as Lia digs into her salad and I'm setting a tomato on my burger, Dad clears his throat. It's only then, as his eyes flash to Mom and he says, "So..." that I realize we've been ambushed.

"I did want to discuss something with you two. Something serious."

Lia looks up and smiles. She's got a spot of dressing at the corner of her mouth. Mom looks at me like, *I'm sorry, but...*

"Matt, it looks like you're not returning to the team, is that right?"

I set my burger down and shake my head, about to ask where this is going, when Dad holds up a hand. "I'm not, this isn't about that, it's... Well, you're not working and you're not on the team. That leaves a lot of time on your hands."

"Why, exactly, are we talking about this now, with..." I look at Lia. "A guest here?"

And if I thought it was uncomfortable then, with Dad gearing up for some kind of speech, I was wrong. Way wrong. It's...

Dad takes a sip of water, wipes his mouth. "Now Lia, with you living on your own, I have to point out the obvious. It might lead to, well, a situation."

Oh, boy. I bury my head. "Dad, please. I'm begging you."

Lia's face flushes, her mouth pulls tight, and her eyes shoot left then right. I can't imagine how red my cheeks are. Even Mom looks uncomfortable. Dad looks around the table. "Look, I was young once, I know how it is."

This is not happening. "Dad, please not now. Please."

"All I'm saying is, Matt, I don't want you inside Lia's house unaccompanied."

As mortifying as it is, it's also silly. "Dad, Lia lives alone. That means I can never go inside? What if she needs help with homework?"

"She can come here."

Lia clears her throat. "Mr. Crosby, if I may?" Soon as she says *if I may* I know I'm sunk. Lia's performing. Her eyes widen, and she transforms into the most innocent little girl in Maycomb. "Matt would never do anything like that. He's been nothing but a gentleman."

Dad nods. "Well, that's good. And I know he is, it's just that well, I'm—"

"Dad, we got it, I'm never to go inside Lia's house, not even to change a lightbulb."

Lia narrows her eyes. "I can change my own lightbulbs, thank you very much."

"Are you sure?" I make a twisting motion. "You have to do it this way."

She sticks her tongue out at me. Mom covers her mouth, about to spit her wine out in laughter.

Dad clears his throat. "Now, I'm serious."

Lia smiles at him, back to innocence now. "I'm sorry, Mr. Crosby."

Dad reaches for the mustard, nods. I can tell he's ready to move on. "It's fine. How's the car running?"

"Really well. Thank you again for everything. Would you like to drive it?"

My dad's eyes brighten. He chews down his burger and nods like crazy. "I would, if that's okay?"

"Of course." Lia stabs her salad. Dad daydreams about the car until Lia's head pops up. "Oh yeah, I took it to get an oil change and the guy at the shop freaked out. He offered to buy it from me on the spot."

I look up. "Really?"

Dad asks where she took it.

"Um, Maycomb Motors, I think?" She tilts her head at me, the way she did when we were kids. "Yes, really. What, are you surprised at my proactive maintenance?"

I nod. "Yes. Changing lightbulbs, oil. I'm surprised at your *proactive maintenance.*"

Dad's brow furrows at Lia, who's busy scrunching her face up at me. "Maycomb Motors? You gotta watch those guys."

I smirk at Lia. I think Dad's jealous she didn't ask him to do it.

Lia shrugs. "Yeah, no. It was fine. I told them it wasn't for sale." She laughs. "Even when he upped the offer, in cash."

I glance at Dad, who shakes his head and mutters something about crooks. At least we're no longer talking about me. My relief is short-lived, as Lia perks up again.

"Oh, and I was thinking, about Mathew not having anything to do. I'm sure we could use him on the set."

I look at her. "*What?*"

She looks me over. "We need some muscle. You would be perfect."

Dad's on board. "Hey, that's not a bad idea. You could use something to do."

Mom gives me a shrug and a smile. Lia stares at me. I know I'm sunk, and so I take a bite of my burger and shrug. "Okay, yeah, sure."

And that's how I joined the set crew for *Garden Variety*.

I WALK Lia home after dinner. She strolls down the middle of the street, her face up, trying to catch leaves as they fall from the trees. I force myself not to keep staring. The way she makes anything extraordinary, how a fall evening becomes her stage.

"So," she spins, misses a leaf, then looks at me. "Feel like digging?"

I shrug. "Well, I can't come inside, so…"

"Ha," she says. Then, all the playfulness leaves her voice. She takes my hand. "Yeah. It might be for the best."

The way she says it makes my chest tighten. My face gets hot. We walk down her driveway and she turns to me, this time serious. "Remember the wedding?"

The wedding in Mr. Higgins' yard, when the bridesmaids abducted Lia and dressed her up and did her hair. She looked like a starlet. My first dance. My first date. I nod my head. "Of course."

She swings my hand up and ducks under with a twirl. "That was the best night."

It was. And then my dad showed up huffing and puffing, arriving to drag me home. "Until the end."

She stops mid-twirl and stares up at me. "Yeah, until the end."

I lean down and kiss her. She kisses me back, gentle at first and then more. I wrap her waist in my arms and she sets her hand on my neck and pretty soon we're lost in the kiss, in the yard, where so much of my life has changed. When she pulls away she's a little out of breath. So am I.

"Yeah, you should definitely not come inside."

From there it's back to work. I grab the shovel and she shows me the latest clue, as she calls it. It's a tattered page, filled with Higgins' cursive scrawl. "'The mirror of light shall lead the way.' This is one of his sermons?"

She nods. "Yes, but guess where I found it?" I stare at her. She drops her shoulders. "Down at the barbeque pit. *Beneath the pines.*"

"Where I was digging?"

"No, well, sort of. It was folded up in the bricks. Crazy, right?"

"Yeah." I look at it again.

Lia grabs my arm and squeezes so hard it hurts. "We're getting closer, Matthew. I checked the mirrors in the house. It must mean something else."

It reminds me of the old Indiana Jones movies Dad and I used to watch together. I glance again at the sermon, her hand on my arm. I try to figure it out, about the mirror and seeing the light and all that. Then, from Corinthians, *"For now we see in a mirror dimly, but then face to face."*

"Hmm, *dimly.*"

Lia slides closer to me. "Face to face."

"So," I look up, toward the woods. "I don't know. This could mean anything. Life, heaven." I take a breath. "Love."

"Such a romantic, Matthew. But no, this is a clue. Higgins made sure I knew there was something to find around here. He's making us work for it."

We look around. And I'm about to lean closer to Lia, wanting nothing more but to kiss her again, when she shoves me off. "Okay, let's get digging."

Chapter 30

Mrs. Morgan welcomes me to the set crew and soon I'm lugging equipment and costumes and otherwise being a gofer. If she's impressed with me being a preseason all-conference (honorable mention) football player, she doesn't show it.

For the next few days, when I'm not hauling trunks of props to the stage, I'm watching Lia put everything into her lines and stage presence. The football bye-week gives me some extra time to think about my decision to quit the team. Is it too late to find Coach and talk about it? Should I at least get down to the field and try?

I don't know, it's easier just to come to the auditorium after school and get lost in the magic of make believe.

Declan is an okay dude. And if I have to admit it, he's good, too. He and Lia have great chemistry, and no one can deny the right two people were cast for Stanley and Rosalina.

I'm right offstage, watching Lia's monologue, when Ryan and Selina nudge me. "Hey, Matt, care to help us?" Selina says.

I jump back. Ryan and Selina laugh. Selina looks out to the stage where Lia is performing and Mrs. Morgan watches with stars in her eyes. "There's no way it's her first play."

"She was part of a comedy troupe thing."

Next thing I know, all three of us are watching her. And as the week goes on, Sarah's watching her too, only now without the glaring. If I didn't know better, I'd think Lia is earning her respect.

On opening night Lia exits costume and makeup, and my feet get tangled. She's wearing what I now know is called a cotton Fiona midi dress—white and fitted before flaring at the calf. She's got her hair pinned up and wrapped. The makeup is perfect, and I can hardly look at her without forgetting my name.

She's nervous, and she keeps reaching for the dog tag, which is now back around my neck because Rosalina Drummond wears pearls and would never dream of wearing such a thing.

She finds me again minutes before she hits the stage. The place is packed with parents and students and faculty. It's crazy to look out and see so many bodies out there.

Lia grabs the dog tag from my chest, her breaths a bit shaky. "I'm going to bomb."

I pull her close, her wide eyes enhanced by the eyeliner, her lips a wild shade of pink. I shake my head. "Lia, you're going to be great. You were made to do this, trust me."

Another peek to the audience. She turns over the dog tag. "I wish my dad was here. To see."

I swallow the lump in my throat, nod. "I'm sure he'd be proud of you. But hey, my mom's watching. And my dad. They're here for you, not me. All I'm doing is hauling around equipment." I duck down to get her attention. "Lia?"

Selena coughs—her new way of telling us to cut it out. Lia smiles at me. One long blink and a couple shaky breaths. "Okay. Okay." She looks to the stage, then back to me. "But hey, I need to talk to you after this."

I roll my eyes with a smile. "Lia, I'm not going treasure hunting tonight."

She smiles, but it doesn't reach her eyes. "I'm serious."

My heart skips a beat. What could she want to talk about? Her mom? It has to be. But I shake it off. Not now, she's got a show to put on. "Okay."

She nods, looks down to her feet, blows out a deep breath. "Okay."

The curtain opens, and Lia transforms. She ambles out to the middle of the stage, to the spotlight, where she turns, finds the faces in the crowd, and opens with her monologue. She is no longer Lia, but Rosalina, long lost and long in love. She's been gone, exiled for a year, and now she's back, to be married to Frank Drummond but longing for Stanley—whom she thought died in the war.

Declan appears, and then I'm lost in their story. To put it short, they bring down the house. Mrs. Morgan sits slightly offstage, beaming. Lia performs like she was meant to perform—like I always knew she'd perform. She doesn't miss a line, delivers them beautifully, precisely, and hilariously when called upon. But she's heartbroken until the end. Even the kiss feels like part of the story. She grabs the audience, and they are happy to be led along.

It's during her ending monologue when Mom meets me just outside. The bouquet is perfect. Twelve long-stemmed roses, wrapped with a shiny bow.

Lia takes a bow, the crowd stands and claps wildly. And it's a strange feeling that comes over me, as I watch her onstage—a feeling that I've seen this before. And I'm in that moment, staring out at her, when I feel a tap on my arm. I turn and find Sarah, giddy and flushed from her performance as Elizabeth.

She looks at me, and I tense up when she smirks at the roses in my hands. I'm ready for the worst, but she only gazes past me and out to Lia. "You know, as Jen's best friend, I still think you're a real jerk." I nod, expecting as much. Sarah fiddles with her necklace, her gaze back to the stage. "But, as a fellow cast member, she is pretty damn amazing. I'll say that much."

I smile at Sarah, who rolls her eyes and turns away. "Nope, you're still a jerk." Then she's gone, following the rest of the cast out to the stage where they join hands and bow. Lia's smile stretches, her hair gorgeously unraveled. She's buzzing from the applause when she comes off stage, sees the flowers and her eyes glisten.

I hand them to her. She stares at them then launches into me for a hug. I whisper in her ear. "I'm so glad you're here."

And then it's busy. A backstage party. Parents introducing themselves, bumping into one another and nodding, everyone smiling. Sarah congratulates Lia because, how could you not? She's the star of the hour. After a while, I find myself tucked away, content but not quite, because I'm so happy for Lia but also kind of sad too because her mom is in jail and her dad is gone and they should be here to see this.

Mrs. Morgan takes the reins and tells the cast how great they were for such a quick turnaround. Then the cast gives the set crew a round of applause, and I'm pulled out of my thoughts to take a bow. And Lia is watching me. I remember she wants to talk, but everyone is swarming her, congratulating her. It's only the first show, we've got three more, two tomorrow and one on Sunday, but she absolutely brought the house down, and I can't wait to see her do it again.

We're in the parking lot when Lia's phone buzzes and she walks away from the hum of parents and cast still raving about the performance. Mom and Dad tell me not to be out too late as they leave. Dad gives me a stern look, reminds me of the No Going Inside rule.

I watch Lia, sniffing the roses and nodding into the phone. Her face still happy but the smile strained some now, pulling away from the post-show glory.

After meeting up with the cast at the Waffle House to celebrate, Lia begs off, and I drive her home where we break the rule. She invites me in with a smile, then wanders into the kitchen. She takes great care to get the roses in a vase. I watch her as she admires them.

I'm looking at the painting on the mantel when she comes in and gives me a hug. Again, she's still glowing, but something is on her mind. I don't want to ruin things by asking her about it, so I sit back as she sets a record on, another one of Higgins' big band tunes, and closes her glossy eyes. I'm sure she's still seeing the audience, hearing the applause. Still blinded by the spotlight. I ask her if she's okay, and she kisses me. I kiss her back and we fall into the couch. There's a new urgency to her kisses, and as much as I enjoy it, it leaves me worried.

Something's happening, but she won't tell me what it is. But the way she's kissing me, breaking the rules, it's sort of hard to think about anything else.

Chapter 31

A double header, in baseball terms. And Lia has huge expectations to meet after last night's performance. I leave her a message to see if maybe she wants to grab some lunch before dress.

It's only a little after ten. I figure she's resting up. The first show is at two this afternoon with the encore at six. It's a big day, and she needs her energy. But the phone call, last night after the show. How she wanted to talk to me. The way she kissed me like she wasn't going to see me again.

With that in mind I run to her house. Run straight down the driveway. The car is gone. Both cars. How? My heart hitches. Linus isn't in his pen. I knock on the door, twice, before pushing it open.

"Lia."

My voice falls flat in the empty house. I look for a note, a freaking clue. Instead I find the roses. Freshly watered, I count eleven. She took one with her.

She can't do this to me again. "Lia."

I search every room, wiping my eyes and muttering to myself, the panic rising from my stomach to my chest. When I get to her bedroom the bed is a tangle of blankets and sheets and pillows. Her bag is gone, because she's gone, I just won't let myself admit it.

I rush back to the porch, run around the house to check the garage. Just in case.

Nothing.

Her guilt won out. She's left to help her mother.

I gather my breath. Walking home I try to think about what she might be doing and how she's doing it. Georgia. That was what she said, right? I try to remember. I have to remember, because this time I'm not letting her do this. Higgins gave her this chance and I can't let her blow it. But first I have to find her.

When I tell Mom she stops cold. I explain how Lia cried at lunch the other day when her mom called. Dad's at work so it's only the two of us, but that's when an idea hits.

"Could Dad find out where her mom is?"

Mom takes a seat and gives it some thought. "Maybe, but Matt, what then? You aren't thinking of going after her, are you?"

I start pacing, like Dad when he's worked up about something. "I don't know, Mom. I can't..."

Mom is back on her feet too, looking out the window. "What about the house? Isn't there a trust? She wouldn't just abandon all that, would she?"

"I don't know. I think she feels guilty, getting all this while her mom is in jail." I remember her crying against me. "Her mom said she was being selfish."

"That's... Lia's the least selfish person I know."

I have a hunch about the Chrysler. And on the way to Maycomb Motors I'm thinking how I need to get in contact with Mrs. Morgan and give her a heads up that her star performer isn't going to be performing today. I look at the clock. Not even twelve hours since I left her last night.

Sure enough, when I pull in the lot at Maycomb Motors I find five guys gathered around the Chrysler Newport. I tear out of the car and charge over to them. *Crooks*, my dad's voice echoes in my head. They're whistling and laughing about something when I approach.

"Hey, excuse me."

They all turn. Two old guys in shiny polo's, tucked in, guts over belts. The other three in coveralls. One of the guys in a polo smiles at me. "Can I help you?"

"Yeah, this car." I nod. "Did a girl come in today?"

He rubs his chin and looks at the others before he grins at me. "Sure did, just brought it in a few hours ago."

"How? Was it titled in her name? Did she say where she was going?" I stop myself from asking more questions and take a deep breath because I'm shaking.

The guy shoots me a look. "I don't... Look, I don't get into personal matters." More looking around. "Take it she's a friend of yours?"

The way he says *friend*. They all sort of chuckle, and I'm ready to start raging. "Yes. She is a friend of mine. And I need to find her."

"Look son, that's not my business."

I nod at the car. "Sure looks like it is." My voice breaks and I look away. The coverall guys are looking around now. Another deep breath to steady myself. "Look, it's really important that I find her."

The old man's face goes somber. "Well, that's just the thing. I don't think she wants to be found."

I'm wasting my time. I'll deal with these guys later. I tell them I know a great lawyer and hustle back to my car. A couple of hours ago, he said. That gives her a head start. To Georgia. That's all I know. But where in Georgia?

Only one way to find out. I get on the road and head for the county jail.

DAD STEPS out to the visitor lobby and looks me over. "Matt. Are you okay?"

It's always strange to see Dad in his officer clothes—all black, boots, utility belt. I hardly ever visit him at work, the jail is a forty minute drive and it's kind of depressing. I turn away from the window, the gleam of razor wire in the distance. "Lia's gone."

"What do you mean, gone?"

We step outside, and I tell him what I told Mom about the phone calls and how Lia was acting last night. When I get to the part about the car I almost think he's going to drive straight over to Maycomb Motors and crack some heads. He, too, wonders about the title and how legit the sale could be. I get him back on track about Lia.

"Dad, I need a favor."

It doesn't take long. In fact, I could have probably done it on my own. Dad looks up Lia's Mom, Ashley Banks. The print out shows two in Georgia. Stetson rings a bell, and I think that might be it.

Dad looks at me closer. "What, you're not thinking of driving down there are you?"

"I really need to find her, Dad."

He nods for us to go back outside. "Matt. I've been extremely tolerant of all this. But you driving to Georgia, that's not going to fly, okay?"

"Dad. I know how it sounds. But this is important. She's throwing everything away."

He looks me over.

I shake my head. "No, this isn't about me. I mean, you know, her life."

Dad nods, gazes out to the towers, the razor wire. "I can't believe she sold the car."

"Please, Dad. I need to do this."

"Matt." I turn to him and he looks around. He's already told me not to go, but something in his face changes. He squints in the sun, wipes the back of his neck, and shrugs. "Be careful, okay?"

I smile. "Yeah. I will, Dad."

The next call isn't easy to make. But I need to get Sarah's number. Jen answers and doesn't tell me to go to hell so it's a start.

I ask how she's doing. "Fine. I um, do need to tell you something, Matt."

I look around, rattled, not really in the mood for any new discoveries. She sighs into the phone. "Austin asked me to Homecoming. I said yes."

I turn my face from the phone as I sigh, but it's more of a release. I nod. "Oh, okay. Yeah."

"It was unexpected, we've been hanging out some, but..."

"Jen, you don't have to explain. Okay? I'm happy for you, really. I'm sorry about how things ended with us, that I wasn't more honest, but I'm...happy, okay?"

"Thanks, Matt."

"Um, so I was actually calling to get Sarah's number."

Her tone goes sharp. "What?"

"No, it's just. I need to get in touch with Mrs. Morgan."

"Oh."

Squeezing the bridge of my nose, I get off the phone with Jen, call Sarah, and tell her the news: that Lia's gone and they're going to need a new Rosalina for tonight, at least.

With all that out of the way, I head home, pack a bag, and tell Mom I'm leaving.

Mom takes me in, the bag slung over my shoulder, heaving with my breaths. I must look crazy. "Matt."

"Mom, I have to find her."

"Matt. I'm supposed to let you drive three states away? What about school?"

"I talked it over with Dad, kind of. I'll be back tomorrow, Mom. Please. Please let me do this."

Her gaze falls to the floor. She bites her lip. When Lia left last time, Mom took it hard, too. She has to know what this means to me. She comes over and hugs me. "Please be careful. Call me."

I hug her back. She turns for her purse.

"Mom, I have money." Which I do, sort of. I cleaned out my stash, and I have maybe a hundred bucks in the bank.

She gives me a credit card. "For emergencies. Call me when you get there and let me know what's going on. I can't believe I'm letting you do this."

I stare at her for a minute. Lia once said how lucky I was to have parents who care about me so much. And it's true, they do care. I am lucky, so lucky. I hug Mom tight and tell her I love her.

And then I take my luck on the road.

Chapter 32

Stetson, Georgia is a little over four hundred miles away. Six hours, maybe less if I push it. But as I head west down I-81 behind an endless line of tractor trailers, the doubt creeps in. What am I doing? What do I plan on saying to Lia when I get there?

I don't know, but as my foot presses down on the gas pedal and the Toyota finds another gear, I suppose I'll figure it out when I get there.

There are other questions. Important questions. Like where in the world am I going? To the jail? My best guess is Lia sold the Chrysler for cash to bail her mother out. But what then?

Miles of white lines pass under the car. Lia mentioned a detox center once when we were digging. And from what I Googled, Stetson seems to be a town of about seven thousand people. There can't be but so many detox facilities in the area.

I change the radio station, tuning out my thoughts and worries. How I've quit football, joined the theater set crew, suffered a concussion, and fallen completely in love. Crazy how forty-five days ago my life was completely in order. Now I'm driving to Georgia without a clue what to do once I get there.

The scenery changes. The mountains are hazy and blue, some early bird trees turning gold as I near Tennessee. The signs for Knoxville are more frequent now, but the landscape does little to soothe my thoughts. This is stupid crazy. I was up for a scholarship. I need to turn around. I could go back to Coach, tell him I'm willing to do what it takes and maybe get back on the field by the time our next game rolls around. A battle ensues.

Turn around.

Can't.

Turn around.

You do and you'll regret it.

I turn up the volume and drive. Escaping. Rescuing. Fleeing. What's the difference? And the whole time I keep a look out, hoping to pass Lia's old Honda, maybe see her on the side of the road. Hoping chance or fate or some sort of luck plays out. But all I see are trucks.

It's nearly six when I arrive.

I FIND the jail a few miles out on the other side of town, near county lines. It's warm, mid-eighties, and as I get out and stretch, it dawns on me that now I have to do all the things I kept pushing out of my mind.

It's freezing in the lobby, the AC cranking as I walk the dingy tiles and wait in line where several downcast glances come my way.

Bail. Bond. Jail sentences and broken families. This place is depressing, and once again I'm reminded of Lia's words about my family.

At the window, the no nonsense lady asks if she can help me. It doesn't take long to find out that yes, Ashley Banks did make bond, an hour ago. But I'm not offered much else. I nod, take a breath, and try to think of my next move—which I don't have yet. There is no next move besides staring at my feet until the speaker crackles and the lady behind the thick glass clears her throat and looks at me for the first time.

"I can't tell you where she is, only that the girl who picked her up was..." The lady grimaces, looks left then right. "You should try the treatment center, the one on Lancaster Avenue."

My head pops up. I crack a smile at the lady and she grimaces. "Good luck."

"Thank you!"

I turn to leave, nearly knocking over a wet floor sign as I scramble to get out of there. Realizing it's probably not in my best interest to be sprinting out of a jail, lobby or not, I slow my steps and nod to the security guard on my way out.

GPS leads me to Valley Views, a facility just south of Stetson, at the very end of Lancaster Avenue, a mostly residential street with big trees and old homes in various condition. The campus is a sprawl of one story buildings that looks like what was an old elementary school. Pulling in, I don't see Lia's Honda and my hope hits the downward drop of the roller coaster I've been riding the entire day.

I park off to the side, with a view of both entrances, but then it feels too sketchy so I move closer to the front. I get out, because I'm sick of the car. The grass has been recently cut and the place is well groomed. Newer doors with locks, flower gardens. I watch a few employees badge the scanner on their way in.

This is good, I'm telling myself. Lia's mom will get the help she needs. But my brain keeps playing the question game. What are Lia's plans? Is she coming back to Maycomb? Last night she was a star—on stage soaking up praise from an adoring crowd. Now, she's bailing her mom out of jail. Bringing her here.

Or maybe she isn't. Again, her car is nowhere to be found, and I have no other options but to wait. The phone rings. It's Mom. I haven't even called.

"Hey, Mom, I'm here."

"Here? Where's here? You were supposed to call."

I picture her pacing, checking the window. "Yeah, I know. Sorry. I'm in Stetson. Safe and sound."

"Oh. Okay good. Did you find Lia?"

I laugh. She's as hopeful as me. "Not yet. I went by the jail. She's bailed her mom out but now I'm at the treatment center. I don't see her car."

"Oh. So listen. I booked you a room at the Red Roof Inn. It's on Tulip Street. Looks like it's close by?"

"Oh, wow. Thanks, Mom." I don't tell her how I hadn't even thought about where I was going to stay.

"I don't know if it's a good idea for you turn around and drive home. But I do want you home tomorrow. And I expect you to call me tonight, once you're checked in. I don't want you on the streets all night."

"Mom, this place is smaller than Maycomb."

"Still." A sigh on her end. "Okay, so what are you going to do, sweetie?"

Now it's my turn to sigh. I run a hand through my hair. "I really don't—"

A scraping sound. Something catches my eye. I turn as Lia's Honda pulls into the entrance. She's alone. Her face is tight and her eyes hollow as she pulls to the curb. In my ear, Mom asks once again if I'm okay.

"Mom, I have to go."

"What is it?"

"Lia's here."

"Oh." Mom starts talking a mile a minute.

"Mom, I'll call you back." I end the call and stand straighter, reminding myself not to charge after her. I wait near my car as Lia looks up, down, sees me and does a double take, her eyes snapping to life.

She's out of the car in a second. "Matthew. What are you doing?"

I start to say everything I've thought about. To spit it all out at once. But there's so much hurt in her puffy eyes, all over her face, as she stands a few feet before me. I've got nothing.

She shakes her head, repeats the question. "What are you doing here?"

I throw my hands out. "I came to see you. I was worried. You just left."

Lia glances back to the car. "How in the world did you find me?"

"You sold the car, Lia? For bail?"

She looks off, her face flushed. "It's not, it's none of your business."

"Lia. Of course it is. I can't let you throw everything away for h—"

She looks at her feet, then back up to me, eyes instantly wet. "For her? For *my mom?* Is that what you're going to say?"

"No, I just..." It's all wrong. This isn't Lia. Her voice is cold, sharp. She's hardened and closed off, a million miles away from the person I know. I look out to the field down the hill from the parking lot. An old baseball diamond, the infield crowded with weeds. I wonder if that's what they do when they get clean—play softball, drink water, and smoke cigarettes. Suddenly, it feels so personal, Lia and her mother and all of their wreckage. The whole trip down, well, it never occurred to me that I have no business being here.

I close my eyes. "Never mind. Look, I'm sorry. I was worried about you. But..."

She sniffles, stands in front of me, arms crossed, eyes mean. Not the girl from the stage or the one from the treasure hunts, but a girl bailing out her mom from jail. She's fighting with all she has to save someone, clawing and clinging to the only family she has left. This girl does not want me here.

"I think I made a mistake."

With nothing else to say, I fiddle with my keys. If I leave now I can make it home by the middle of the night. I hesitate, look back to her once more, still wanting to help, still searching for the light in her eyes, eyes I've dreamed about every night for the past few years. "Okay, sorry, Lia. I'll leave."

She's clutching her sides, tears scraping down her cheeks. "You should, Matthew. You've quit football, your job, everything. You need to go back to your life."

I stop and laugh, throw my hands up. "Honestly, I do kind of miss football."

I don't know why I say it, but Lia wipes her eyes, stares at her feet. "I know you do." She looks up, her voice returning to normal, if only a little. "And you're good at it. Good enough to go to college."

I turn all the way around to her. Take a step closer. "Lia, you're good enough too."

She shakes her head. More wiping at her face. But I might as well say it all, while I'm here. "At theater. You're amazing. You saw them last night. And Mrs. Morgan said it's fine, that you have a place in any production you want. You're that good, Lia."

She squeezes her eyes tight to stop the dam. Her voice cracks. "Why can't you just let me do this? Why do you care so much?"

I'm right in front of her now. "What?"

"Why?" Her face breaks open. Her endless tears stream from her eyes and she wipes them away. It does no good. She's falling apart, and all I want to do is wrap her in my arms, but she shakes her head. Her hair down, shirt wrinkled, her hands shaking. If ever there was a time for a confession, for the truth, it's now. I look into her eyes. "Because I care about *you*, Lia. I care so much. I love you."

The last part kind of tumbles out. She looks up at me, then quickly glances off, her chin quivering. She covers her face with her hands and her shoulders shake. Then she falls into me, sobbing and warm.

No one seems to notice. Unlike school, Valley Views is a place where you can hug all you want. It's encouraged. We hold each other like that for a while. By the time she pulls away and sniffles, she's a little bit more of the Lia I know again. She backs off but looks up to me with something akin to a smirk.

"When did you decide that?" She wipes the corner of her eye with a finger. "That you, love me?"

I look around. "Three years ago. Just now. Somewhere in between."

She reaches out for my hand, the smile getting away from her now. Her eyes are wrecked. Another look toward the building. The rows of windows. "I can't go to college." She looks to the building, her thoughts wading in excuses. "Or leave her."

"Lia, I know it's your mom, but you can't throw everything away trying to save her. You've done the right thing getting her here. But none of her choices are your fault. At some point, and I hate to say this, your mom has to help herself."

She shoots me a look.

I shrug. "What, it took me six hours to come up with that."

Lia rolls her eyes but doesn't let go.

I try to seal the deal. "Mr. Higgins left you an opportunity. Take it."

A plane drones overhead. Birds chirp. She lets out a deep, wet breath. "I suppose there is the treasure."

I laugh. "Yeah, the treasure."

She falls back into me and whispers, "I love you too."

And I'm so glad I came.

Chapter 33

I call Mom from the hotel. My trip isn't a complete bust. Lia is going to meet me here at nine, after visiting hours at Valley Views. I'm talking a mile a minute, until I realize I probably should have kept my big mouth shut.

Mom stops me. "She's staying with you. In a hotel room?"

"Well..."

"Matthew, sweetie. Listen closely, okay. I'm so thrilled you were able to find her, talk to her, and hopefully convince her to come home. But Lia cannot stay with you in a hotel room. I'm not *that* cool."

"Where she's supposed to stay?"

I hear rustling in the background. Mom in her purse. "I'll book another room, right now."

"Oh, um, okay."

"Matthew Crosby. You are not to sleep in the same hotel room as Lia. Am I absolutely clear?"

"Mom. Yes. I got it."

I grab some fast food and get back to the hotel where I flip through channels. The next two hours feels like years. At ten minutes after nine there's a knock at the door. I leap to my feet and fling it open. Lia stands before me, messy and gorgeous. She bites her lip.

"Room service."

Her eyes are puffy from crying. Her hair is all over the place. And yet she's trying hard to keep it together. I invite her in and she looks around, takes a seat on the other bed. I sit across from her. "So, my mom booked you a room."

"Why?" She looks up, then over to the bed. "Oh."

"Um…"

She smiles, flops herself back on the mattress. "Yeah."

I ask how it went. She throws her arms out, stares at the ceiling, her chest rising and falling. "Well, I just paid two thousand dollars cash for a one month deposit." She glances at me, then back to the ceiling. "So yeah, I sold the car."

I nod. "My dad's crushed."

She sighs, on the verge of more tears but fighting through it. She sets her hands on her stomach. "Rehab's not cheap. This is her third stint at one of these places, but… She's eating. She promises to try. She said I was the best daughter in the world." Her voice cracks, she loses the battle with herself. "And then she asked how much money I had left."

I take a seat on the bed, bow my head. "Lia, I'm so sorry."

She grabs at the bedspread, squeezing the pain from her eyes. "Not, 'I love you, Lia. Thanks for dropping everything.' Not, 'How's your life?' So that I could tell her I landed the lead role in the play and crushed it on opening night, got a standing ovation and a handsome, too-good-to-be-true boy brought me flowers. Nope, just, 'How much cash?'"

We wrestle with the silence in the cheap hotel room. All I can do is whisper I'm sorry and watch as she licks her wounds once again, like she always has done. She rubs the dog tag, and I know she's wishing her father were still alive so he could help her, hug her, love her, and tell her how proud he is of her. At some point I scoot beside her and stretch out. She curls in to me and cries.

I think my mom would understand.

I WAKE up in the middle of the night. The streetlight cuts through the part in the curtains. I still have my shoes on. Lia's still cuddled beside me, eyes closed and her lips almost curled into a smile.

I think about back home. My life with Lia, without Lia, all of it together. What I told her about football was true. I do miss it, been missing it. It just took me some time away from things to realize it.

Besides, I'm good at football. I want a scholarship. Everything I told Lia about her life and future applies to me, too. I have to take my own advice.

Lia stirs, breaking my thoughts. She has a house and a small trust fund. Not sure if it's enough to pay for college, but it's a start. She can get scholarships, Mrs. Morgan can help. From one night on the stage, everyone in that auditorium knows where she belongs. We can do this, there can be a happy ending. Or maybe I'm just an optimist.

She wakes me up at seven with a kiss on the lips. I blink to life and she laughs. "Hi."

"Hi."

She leans forward, her forehead on mine. "I guess we didn't get the other room?"

"What other room?"

She slaps my chest and rolls out of bed. Watching her stretch, it reminds me of another night we spent together, when we were fourteen and fell asleep on the dock down at Greer Pond. Mom caught me in the morning, and I would've been grounded had it not been for Lia's birthday and crazy baptism in the little pond. But now, as her shirt rises and I see a glimpse of her flat stomach in the morning sun, well, this is different. Way different.

Her arms fall to her sides. She starts for the window. "Well, I've got to go see Mom."

I search her face to see how she's feeling. Her head is up, it's the go-getter Lia. The one you can't deny. I wipe my face. "And then?"

She throws open the curtains and the room flashes bright. Gone is any sign of last night's hopelessness. Her eyes are lit with the new day. With fearlessness.

"Well, it's day one of her new life," she says in a deep voice. She nods, as though forcing herself to believe this time it's going to work.

I set my feet to the floor. "Okay, and Lia, I'm happy for you, really. But again, I think you should get back to Maycomb and finish the year." I realize I sound like my dad. I rub my eyes, stand up. "You were so good in that play."

I'm expecting her to lash out, to snap at me. But she doesn't, she turns and smiles. "Thank you. I want to come back, I do. But I need a few days. Maybe a week to whip her into shape. There's an old neighbor, a sweet lady, Mrs. Patterson, she has a room she can rent me. Mom's got six weeks of treatment. Then..." she shrugs. "I don't know. We'll see. Maybe she can come live with me."

Before I can process what she's saying, my phone buzzes, sliding across the table.

MOM CALLING

Damn. She's probably figured out no one checked into the other room. Lia looks at the phone, then to me. "Might want to get that."

I shake my head, run a hand through my hair. "I can't, not now."

She walks over to me and wraps her arms around my neck. "Look, Matthew. Drive home. See your parents. Call your coach. I'll be back in a few days, a week, I think. I have to make sure she gets over the hump. I need to do this, okay?"

Her eyes are wide and sincere. All I can do is nod. She sets her head against me. "And I need you to feed Fremont."

"And Linus and the ducks and..."

"Shut up." She shoves me on the bed. My phone buzzes in protest. I grab her and we roll to her side.

"See, you have to come home. What about your farm?"

Lia's lips part with her smile. "Yeah." She shifts, up on one elbow. "I am coming back, Matthew. I know you're worried it will be like, you know."

"Like last time?"

She looks to the ceiling. "Yeah. But if I can get her through this, have her come back with me..."

Again, I want to tell her the odds are not in her favor. She's setting herself up to get hurt again. I hate to see her throw everything away. And the talk of her renting a room kills me. But seeing how much it means to her, how she's so wrapped up in believing this time it's going to work, I don't have the heart to prepare for 'just in case.' She's leaped out of a plane without a parachute.

She slides her hand up my arm. "And don't think I don't know what you're thinking, Matthew."

"Huh? What, I was thinking about breakfast."

"Yeah okay," she laughs. "The two most honest people in the world share a hotel room, there's bound to be trouble." She looks off and sighs. "When I told my mom about the house, her eyes lit up. She asked about you."

"Really?" I'd never formally been introduced to Lia's mom, only seen her a few times in the neighborhood.

"Seriously. My mom knows how much you mean to me."

I've never once considered this. Lia and her mom talking about me. Lia thinking of me for the past three years when she was out West or traveling or doing adventurous Lia things.

"But," she says, thinking it through. "I'm hopeful, but not stupid. I can't trust her yet. And yes, I know how it sounds, but I need to be sure she's better first."

"So what..." I try to rephrase it. "I mean, what kind of drugs does she do?"

Lia shrugs. "Wine, weed, pills. But if she can get a hold of some coke now...whoa boy, watch out."

I wish I hadn't asked, hearing Lia rattle off the list so casually. Not for the first time, I wonder how she ever survived and became what she is coming from such an environment.

Between the hopeful glimmer in her eyes, the lilt in her voice, there's nothing else to say. I take her hand. "I really don't want to leave you. What about the car? The Honda. Will it make it back?"

"It's never failed me before. And you should get home. I never wanted to drag you into this." She nods to the phone, buzzing for the third time in an hour. And with that, Lia is on her feet, turning to the mirror and wiping her hair back, fixing her shirt. She's got all the answers and she's looking all too ready to leave.

"Okay," I say. "See you soon?"

She smiles. "Yes. Soon."

I walk over to her. "Wait, how about breakfast first?"

She smirks at me. "Are you trying to prolong this?"

"Prolong what? I'm hungry." I slide my hands around her waist. She reaches up and sets a hand in my hair. Then she turns her head and kisses me full on the lips.

"Okay. I guess I could go for some pancakes."

Chapter 34

It takes everything I've got to leave her. But after she drives off, one phone call to Mom is all it takes to reel me into reality. She picks up on the first millisecond of the first ring.

"Matt. No one checked into the room."

"Mom, please trust me. Please?"

"Trust you? Are you saying she stayed with you? What's going on?"

"Mom, I'm getting ready to leave now. Lia's staying for a few more days, or something."

Her voice softens, but only a little. "Is she okay?"

"I think so," I sigh. "Her mom wants money."

"Oh, dear."

"But I think I talked her into coming back. Sticking it out at school. Going to college, or something." I try to butter her up, move away from the hotel room stuff. "I sounded a lot like you and Dad there."

"And you two shared a hotel room?"

"Mom, it was nothing like that. She was a mess." I squeeze the bridge of my nose. "Okay, I'm leaving soon. I'll be home, uh, this afternoon, hopefully."

"Okay, we'll talk then. Be careful, Matt."

I end the call, appreciating my mother more than ever after seeing the damage Lia's mother has caused. I turn the key and get up the road.

I spend the long drive back working things out in my head. How I'll get my place back on the team, make amends with Coach and my teammates. I've missed some games and way too much practice, but a lot of that was technically protocol. Lia will return and get back onstage. I can do both, have some of my old life, and some of this new life. I don't know why I ever thought I couldn't.

But my worry for Lia only grows with each mile I put between us; I see the doubt creeping into her face at breakfast. How she wants so badly to make it work. To help her mom stop…being what she's always been, and they can finally have what she wants so badly. I can't bear to think what it will do to her if it doesn't work out. It would break her in half.

Mom's at the door when I walk in the house. Her mouth is tight and her face is strained with worry. A swift look at her nails and they're gnawed to the quick.

She gives me a quick hug. "How was the drive?"

"Long."

"And Lia? She's okay?"

I shrug and take a big breath. "Yeah, as good as she can be. She's convinced herself this time it will work."

Mom leads me to the table. I take a seat, and she pulls out lasagna, serves up a big, cheesy square, and sets the plate in front of me. Again, I have a new appreciation for my parents. "Thanks. Dad at work?"

Mom sits beside me, abandoning her paperback. She sets her reading glasses on the table. "Yeah. So this place, it's a rehab facility?"

"Yeah, it's like her third time trying to get clean. Between bail and rehab Lia's already sunk the car money." I take a bite and burn my tongue. I'm too hungry to care. I only stopped for gas once and to use the bathroom at a rest stop. I just now remember I didn't eat.

Mom's face looks pained. She shakes her head. "That poor girl."

I tell her everything about the trip, about Valley Views. And as I grab up seconds I even tell her about my plans to get back on the field. She says she'll support my decision, then with a smile adds, "Although I did support your decision not to play a tiny bit more."

Later that evening, I walk down to Higgins' place to feed Linus and Fremont and find Mr. Wood chugging along in the field on his riding lawnmower. I make my way over to him and he kills the engine. I say hello and he grunts.

"Someone had to cut the grass," he says, flicking his eyes to me like it's my fault it's not cut.

I nod, unsure what to say besides, "Looks good."

"Yeah." He pulls out a rag, wipes his face, and looks around, admiring the precision swipes he's made along the field. Just when things start to get awkward, he turns back to me with a squint. "She okay?"

A two word question that's impossible to answer. I fight over what to say when Mr. Wood nods a few times. "Yeah, well, she came over one evening, to introduce herself. She stayed for a while in the den with Carol. They must have spent an hour talking about knitting and such. Anyway, haven't seen Carol that giddy in years."

"Really?" I turn to the house and swallow the lump in my throat. I picture Lia knocking on the door, charming the gruff old neighbors. Then I realize Mr. Wood is still waiting for my answer. I do my best with it. "Yeah, she's okay. Went to visit family."

"Ah, that's good."

With that, he cranks up the mower. I head for the house. Inside, everything looks in order, or, in Lia's order, anyway. I feed the cat and walking out, I pause to look at the painting. Of us. Younger us, in the sunset. Then I force myself to turn away and lock up. I leave the key under the pot like she said and wave to Mr. Wood. He doesn't bother to wave back.

Lia calls at nine that night, after visiting hours. She's still upbeat, telling me about how she talked her mom into picking up all that trash around the baseball field.

I fall back on my bed, wipe my face, and stare at the ceiling as Lia tells the story of picking up litter with all the excitement of a trip to an amusement park.

"Oh, and guess what? She was asking about the house. I told her about the treasure and Linus—minus the part about biting Tyler, and, hey did you feed Free?"

"I did, he says hello." I tell her about Mr. Wood mowing the grass.

"Aww, that's so sweet. Carol and I are going to knit up some scarves. Do you want one?"

I close my eyes. "Yeah."

She takes a breath. "Thanks again."

"Of course."

"No, really. Not just that. For everything. For coming all the way down to Georgia to check on me."

I laugh. "I do make a good detective."

"Yeah. You make a good lots of things."

I smile. Lia sighs. I sigh. "I'm going to miss you tomorrow. And your freshmen buddies are going to be devastated."

She giggles. "Poor things. Hey, I was thinking, I might call the school and see if they will send my assignments."

I sit up. "Lia, that's great." It's a sign she might stick it out. With school and hopefully everything.

"Yeah, and that way I can keep up with my studies. Listen to me, *my studies.*"

"No, yeah, I can go to the office and talk to guidance, if you want? Get some info."

"Yeah, okay. That would be nice." She yawns.

"I can let you go. I'm sure you're beat."

Another yawn. "Yeah, but will you stay on, for just a bit more?"

"Of course."

Chapter 35

I wake up early, fully charged and ready to make changes. I get to school an hour before first period and head to the front office to get some info for Lia. Only guidance doesn't come in until ten minutes before school starts apparently so I'm left with my next chore, finding Mrs. Morgan.

She's in her office near the auditorium. A world away from the rest of the school. I knock gently, find her sipping coffee, the gentle hum of NPR in the background. When she doesn't answer, I knock again and she turns—the annoyance on her face quickly shifting to intrigue. I wonder what Sarah has told her about Lia.

"Matt, good morning."

"Good morning. I just wanted to come by and talk about Lia."

She gestures to a seat near her desk. "Ah, yes. I'd love to hear this."

Ouch. Not quite what I was expecting. Only now do I really think about the show. "Um, how did it go? Saturday, and yesterday?"

Another sip before she sets her mug down. She leans back in her chair. There must be a million flyers on the wall from plays of all over the world. Probably reprints, although with Mrs. Morgan, who knows. She's only been here a year, and she's stood out since the day she arrived. Sort of like someone else I know.

"How did it go, you ask?" She tilts her head. "Well, it went, I suppose. We got through all three plays without major incident."

"Well, that's good, right?"

She shrugs. A dramatic, stage shrug. "Good. Fine. Okay." She pouts. "Yes, it was all very *okay*. How's Lia?"

"She's still in Georgia. It's sort of a family emergency. I'm supposed to be getting her assignments and stuff, not sure how long she's going to be down there."

"Ah, but you await her return?"

"I...yeah." Who talks like this? Well, Lia does, I suppose. And worldly drama teachers. I notice she's wearing a scarf and it reminds me of Lia knitting.

I smile. My gaze falls to my lap, then I feel Mrs. Morgan still eyeing me with almost a smirk. "So." I shift in my seat. "Um, I was wondering, for Lia, if she would be able to get another shot. Be in another play? This whole thing, it really isn't her fault. She's actually pretty selfless, to leave the show—she had to do it, and—"

Mrs. Morgan's hand slowly comes up, and I stop talking. Outside, some landscapers buzz by on mowers, otherwise, it's a bit secluded. This part of the school doesn't come to life until after lunch. Mrs. Morgan sighs. "Matt. I've been involved with plays, drama, features, basically my entire life." She gestures around the room to the flyers. "Without telling you my age, dear, let's just say I've seen my share of characters, both onstage and off. Understand?"

Not at all, lady.

For a moment she's lost in the flyers. Then she returns to the room, her sharp gaze settling on me. "I returned to Maycomb to give back to the community. To slow down. But I never thought I'd see, hmm, how do I say this? Matt, in my lifetime, I've seen maybe three actors who have what Lia brings to a stage." She holds up her fingers. "Three."

I smile again. I can't help it. I've always known how special Lia is, but to hear this sophisticated, albeit strange lady gushing about her is something else.

She sets down her hands. "I assume you know exactly what I mean, am I right?"

Her curved grin makes me squirm. Thankfully she moves on. "Whatever her personal trouble may be, I hope she is well. I do hope she gets it taken care of. As for her returning to our little productions, it goes without saying. We will be doing eight or nine of them this year, so there's plenty of opportunities. But even without them, I am willing to make recommendations," she holds up one spindly finger, "after her one performance mind you, to any school in the country. That said, she's going to need more of a resume." More grinning. "It's why I did some digging."

"Digging?"

"In rehearsals one day I asked Lia about her acting, what experience she had. She mentioned a comedy troupe."

I nod furiously. "The Pinwheel thing? Yeah."

Mrs. Morgan smiles at me. "Yes, the Pinwheel Comedy Troupe. They're very popular in the northwest. I found their YouTube page."

I start to say something, but she cuts me off.

"She's remarkable, Matt. I want her not only in my plays, but the Maycomb Players, as well as the troupe in Roanoke."

"Wow, really?"

"Of course. She's a natural, for lack of better a term. She has *it*, as they say. Something special. Looks, charisma, stage presence, and a hint of quirkiness that makes her approachable. She's...well again, you know all this, right?"

"Well, I..."

"Yes, of course you do, it's all over your face. Now, what about you? Are you still with our set crew, or..."

"Well, I may be back on the football team, so..."

She rolls her eyes. "Ready to get back to bashing your head again, huh? Well, so long, Matthew."

I laugh until she spins back to her desk and gets back to her laptop.

"Oh, okay." I get to my feet, looking back to her one more time. "Um, bye?" Then I let myself out.

I don't hear a thing said in class. I need to tell Lia she has more to do. I want to relay every word Mrs. Morgan had to say about her. I slide by guidance at lunch, because I'm not yet ready to sit with my former, maybe still, teammates, and the Jen/Austin thing might be a little awkward for a while.

Ms. Jackson in guidance is all too eager to help. I lay it on thick, tell her what I can without saying "rehab" as I let her know Lia needs her assignments and plans to return shortly. But without Lia calling herself, there isn't much she can do. I assure her I understand, and I make a note to be sure Lia gets right on that.

She stops me on the way out. "Matt, in the meantime, if she needs to talk to someone—here." She digs in her bag and gets me a card with her name and number. "About anything."

I take the card. "Thanks."

It's crazy how the school seems emptier without Lia. Even as we didn't have classes together I guess knowing she was around—in the halls, outside with the freshmen, in the auditorium—gave me a comfort I didn't realize until now.

I get through the day and head for the football field. I'm first, as I'm not dressed out because I want to talk to Coach first. He sees me coming and does a double take.

"Hey, Coach."

"Crosby, what are you doing down here?"

I shrug, look out to the field where I've spent so much time the past couple of years, lost in the haze of grass and dirt, the spurt of the whistle. "Did some thinking. I want to play, if you'll still let me?"

He glances at Coach Wills who smiles, before he turns back to me. "You've missed two games, practice too."

"I know. I realize I've lost my spot, but still. I can practice, if it's okay?"

He looks me over. "You're all cleared?"

I nod, kind of a lie but not really. "Yeah. I'm good."

"Well, go dress. And hurry."

The guys are weird at first. Austin kind of tip-toeing around me until I catch him at the water cooler.

"Hey, Austin."

"Oh, uh, hey, Matt."

"I told you," I say with a smile. "I'm cool with you and Jen, or whatever."

He looks at me, wipes his mouth with his arm. "She said you called. Lia okay?"

"I think so. So look, let's try to play some ball and quit acting weird, okay?"

He laughs. "Yeah, okay. You good, the noggin and all?"

I shrug, pull my helmet on. "Good as ever."

With that settled, I get in some reps with the second team, Coach's way of punishing me for missed time, I guess. I'm fine with it, with moving and running and even the hitting. It gives me something to do, gives my body a purpose, and I don't think about Lia every two minutes. Maybe every ten.

After school my body is tired. A good kind of tired. I drive home with the windows open, the wind in my hair, thinking about practice, how it felt to be back on the field—until I pull down the street and my heart skips a beat.

Lia's Chrysler sits in our driveway, its doors open, the trunk and the hood popped. Dad stands off to the side, staring at it like it's a present under the Christmas tree.

Oh wow. He actually did it.

Chapter 36

I park and leap out of the car.

Dad turns his proud smile on me. "Hey, did you practice today?"

I nod, gesture to the car. "Dad? What's going on?"

He crosses his arms, forearms the size of fence posts. "I went and saw those crooks down at Maycomb Motors, that's all. How was it? Practice?"

My face cracks open with a smile. "You bought the car back?"

He throws a shoulder up. "Kind of, not really. I told them the sale wasn't legal. Lia's seventeen, I asked to see the title and threatened to make some calls. They were ready to make a deal."

I shake my head, turning to the car, then back to Dad. "Really?"

"Yeah, gave them what they gave her."

I would have never guessed Dad would come to Lia's rescue. While I knew the guy had softened up some, this was unbelievable. Then again, he does love that car. He slaps me on the back. "How was it being back on the field? Are you cleared?"

"Well, I should probably go talk to Dr. Stinnett, but yeah, mostly. It was good." I look at the car, the chrome shining in the evening sun. "Hey, Dad, listen. Lia spent the money. She paid for her mom to go to...you know."

He looks to the car, then to me. "Well, we can work that out, the two of us. Either way, I can't let those guys get away with robbing her like that. This car is worth triple what they gave her, at least."

For the next few days I fall back into an old routine, only with some new wrinkles. Football practice, feeding Lia's animals, waiting for her to call with updates. School isn't bad, still lonely, but not like it was. I see Mrs. Morgan and tell her I'll pitch in with the set stuff when I can, and she simply calls me a caveman. I don't think she's kidding.

I casually move back to the lunch table. Jen sits with Austin and it's mostly not weird, even though I still want to break Tyler's neck for what he said. But mostly we talk football, soccer, that sort of thing.

Sarah shakes her head, gushing about her turn playing Rosalina, then shrugs and says she did her best, having to follow up Lia's performance. "So how is she, anyway?"

The entire table looks up and awaits my answer. People know she's gone. A girl like Lia does not go unnoticed. And now they come to me for answers. At least the rehab thing has managed to stay out of the rumor mill. Family emergency is honest and leaves a lot more to the imagination.

"Oh, well, she's still helping her mom, so I'm not sure when she's getting back."

Sarah, picking at her salad, glances at Jen, whose face still goes tight at the mention of Lia's name. "Oh, well I hope the best for her. There are still like a bunch more plays when she returns."

"Yeah," I say, and leave it at that. Everyone watches me without looking at me. It's like they know I'm heartbroken. I'm not sure I can sit in the cafeteria, amongst the carefree noise and chatter, and play along that I'm the same Matt Crosby as before. I tell myself not to worry, she'll be back. We talk on the phone, this isn't like last time. But my heart drops and my stomach sinks and it's hard to convince myself she hasn't done it all over again.

But I have to prepare for it. For a big FOR SALE sign to go up down at Higgins' place, for a truck to come and pick up Linus. For Dad to keep the Chrysler and I'll have to see it in the driveway but I'll never drive it because if I do I'll only picture Lia behind the wheel, her breathtaking smile, her glittering eyes, crazy notions spilling from her lips. I'll picture all that and feel the empty hope she'll return every time.

So I slowly take steps. And as the first week goes by, with two phone calls from Lia, her voice breaking with happiness because her mom's doing great and thinking about working again and isn't this amazing. I tell her it is. It's amazing.

When I tell her Dad got the car back she screams into my ear. I laugh, give her the details. Tease her about how she'll have to steal it from Dad to get it back.

I get her caught up at school. I gently remind her what Mrs. Morgan said, about all the plays and how she's got her pick of any part she wants. Then I tell her how great she is, top three on her little list, and Lia squeals every time and makes me repeat it again. And so I keep going; I tell her again and again. I remind her that she could go to college, and maybe make a living acting, and Lia sighs and says "that would be great," but she says it in the way you would say going to the moon would be great.

I want it to be enough to convince her to come back, but I can tell it's not. She's staying with Mrs. Patterson and it's only a few miles from Valley Views and to me it's beginning to sound more and more permanent. And I should be happy for her, but I can't. I'm too selfish.

When she asks what's wrong, I tell her nothing, I'm happy for her, really. And then she yawns and tells me she misses me. And I tell her I miss her too, but I don't tell her I miss her so much that it hurts. And as her yawns get longer and our conversation slows, we listen to each other breathe. Again I remind myself not to be selfish, not to weigh her down. Not to keep telling her how much she means to me. After a while, when I think she's fallen asleep, she takes a quick breath.

"Matthew?"

"Yeah?"

"I really hope it works this time, you know?"

"Yeah. Me too, Lia." And I do hope it works out. Of course I do. At least I want to believe that I want it to work because otherwise it makes me a terrible human being. And that's not what I want to be, especially with Lia.

And we end it like that. I promise to call her tomorrow and she says she and her mom are going fishing in the little pond in the woods. "Can you believe it? Mom fishing?"

I can believe it. With Lia I believe anything, because that's what she does to me, she makes me feel like I can be myself and it's okay.

MOM HAS me go to Doctor Stinnett so she can officially clear me to play. She does this by sitting me down, looking me in the eye as she sits across from me, hands in her lap, and asking if I'm ready to play. I tell her I'm good and she nods.

By Friday night I'm focused. Coach says I'm not starting but will play. Eric hops in place, eager and ready to charge out to the field.

We played Hanford twice last year, so I'm familiar with what they like to do. So while everyone is expecting me to pout and mope about a sophomore taking my place, I hustle over to him. "You good?"

He jerks his face to me. "Yeah."

"Cool." I give him some pointers, starting with Karson Jenkins, the too quick linebacker I remember so well from last year. "He'll try to level you on the first play, set the tone. So be ready for that, hit him first and show him you're not scared."

Eric's eyes widen in surprise. Great, now I've scared him.

I smack his shoulder pads. "Either way, the only thing to do is go out there and mix it up, get over the jitters."

The cool chill in the night air. The cheers, the hits, the whistle. It comes back quickly. Only we're down 17-10 at the half, and Coach is ticked because we've fumbled twice. My replacement coughed it up once on the opening drive, when Jenkins popped him after a five yard catch. I hope it wasn't my fault, that I scared him with my advice, but either way, it's done now.

Coach finally finishes chewing us out. He glances my way. "Crosby, you're in on the first possession."

Austin and Aiden make a big deal out of this, smacking my

helmet. *That's what I'm talking about* and all that. I set my helmet on and strap up. I just want to play.

This was my life before Lia. Being good at football. Being big, solid, reliable, Ken Crosby's son, the kid who worked at Yearly Farm and Garden. So I'll be that guy tonight. What else do I have to do?

It works. Even after missing so much time, I quickly fall into the groove and get a couple of good blocks in on Jenkins. He talks some trash but I tune it out.

We tie things up in the third, but Hanford scores on a trick play. From there we manage a long drive, and I catch a ten yard pass for a first down and we go on to even it up again. But just when it seems like a back and forth, both defenses make some stops. We punt, they punt. A dog fight ensues.

Late in the fourth quarter, with the score still tied, I get open on a hitch route and Austin zips the ball across the field. I secure the catch at the twenty, spin off a defender and gallop down the field. I'm at the five and have the angle when instead I lower my head and plow into a corner back. Our helmets clack and I bull my way into the endzone. The crowd erupts, the band crashes into the fight song.

I spike the ball and throw my hands up to the sky. Mrs. Morgan was right.

I am a caveman.

Chapter 37

It's all smacks on the back and head in the locker room. Coach even manages a smile as he lauds our focus and never-quit attitude. It feels good, too, to be back in the mix, to be the hero, so to speak. To release the breath I sucked in over a month ago.

Aiden talks me into a party afterwards, in someone's house I don't know. It's loud, crowded, and as soon as I walk inside I'm ready to leave.

Jen finds me in the kitchen. "Great game, Matt."

She smiles the old smile at me, the one fueled by sports and high school and all the things she loves. She looks good, in jeans and a fitted NorthFace jacket. It's nice to see her happy again.

I nod. "Thanks, Jen."

"Matt is the man!" Austin, beer in hand, comes up and sets an arm around her.

I nod again. It was a good game, five catches for seventy-two yards and a touchdown in one half of play. I should be thrilled, I expect to start again next week. Instead I keep checking my phone. No call from Lia.

Jen sees me and frowns. "So, how's Lia?"

Lia's name comes out awkwardly. Or maybe it's just awkward with my ex-girlfriend saying Lia's name. Either way I pocket my phone and shrug. "She's good." I nod too many times. Repeat it again. "She's good."

The song changes in the living room. Everyone screams. A reunion takes place as two girls clash into each other for a hug. They jog in place and squeal. We watch for a minute before Jen glances at Austin. "I heard that Lia's Mom, is like..."

"She's sick. That's all. Lia is helping take care of her."

More glancing. Jen tilts her head. "Yeah. Well, I hope she gets better."

"Me too." I take a breath and point to the back door, where the deck is full of people, more people to tell me I'm the man, tell me how great I am. "Look, I gotta run, uh..."

And it's with that sort of grace that I exit out the back, where people start cheering and being dumb. It's clear I'm the one who has changed. This used to be enough for me, to score the winning touchdown. To be the hero.

But it's not now, all that's changed thanks to Lia, who's gone.

I call her twice on the way home. The second time I leave a stammering voicemail. "Hey, uh, I was checking in to see..." I wince at my own words. "Anyway, we won and..." Like she cares. "Um, so give me a call when you can." Great, now I'm making whiney demands.

I drive past my house, down to Higgins', where everything is quiet and in order. I let myself in to feed Fremont. I turn on the lamp as he circles me, in and out of my legs, and I wonder if I'll take him if she...

I don't allow myself to finish the thought.

"She'll be home soon, I think," I say to Fremont as he leads me to the dish. I pour some food for him, and I know I should leave and not be some weird stalker guy, but it's hard. The place is no longer Higgins' but Lia's. It smells like her; her clothes are on the couch. Her stupid treasure maps are all over the place.

I do my best not to look at the mantel, but eventually my eyes make the trip. I look at the two kids—us—side by side on the dock. The glow of the evening sun on the water. "So is this what you had in mind, Preacher, bringing us together again?"

My eyes blur, and I shake my head, cursing myself for falling in all over again.

I leave the lamp on and turn for the door. I lock up behind me, wiping my eyes one last time.

DAD WAKES me up at seven-thirty the next morning. He's holding the paper and the smile on his face crinkles his eyes. "You made the front page!"

I lift my head from the pillow. "Really? What time is it?"

"What time is it?" Dad mimics. "Matt, look, you made the front page."

Maycomb Takes Down Hanford. There's me, frozen mid-stride, having steamrolled that poor cornerback en route to the endzone.

"Cool." I set my head back down and Dad stands at my door.

His smile drops with the newspaper to his side. "You okay?"

"Yeah, tired. It's exhausting making the front page."

"Ha, I'll say. Okay, get some rest, but not too late. I need some help with a few things."

I sigh. Even the front page can't save me from Dad and his chores.

First thing I do is check my phone. Nothing from Lia. Two from Aiden asking why I bounced so early. Oddly enough there's one from Jen about how it was good to see me.

I tell myself I will not be a lump. That yeah, sure, it took me a year or two, (or three, if I'm honest), to get over Lia, but I'm not doing that again. Even though she has a house here and may be coming back. Instinctively I reach for the dog tag that is no longer there. I laugh it off and get myself out of bed. She's coming back, again. I know it.

I find Dad in the Chrysler, where else? He's taken the panel off and his hair is crazy. He's got the multimeter out. "Need to replace this plastic washer fix shaft."

"Um, okay."

I've never seen my dad like this. He's a kid, leaping out, wiping his hands. "Probably going to need to search online." He looks over the car, eyes filled with wild pride that I think is for the car until he sets a hand on my shoulder. "Just wow, Matt. You played a helluva game last night."

"Yeah."

"So, that touchdown? You really laid that kid out."

"I know, I—"

"No, it's okay. But usually you get an angle, you take off. You're fast, and after the concussion I was a bit surprised, you know?"

I stare at my feet, wondering when my dad became so intuitive. "Yeah, well, honestly? Something sort of broke inside me, I can't explain it."

He grimaces, wipes his hand on his shirt. "But you're feeling all right, the head and all?"

"I am. I suppose. Thinking a lot about Lia. I'm worried about her, you know?"

He nods. "I know. She's something else, I'll say that. When I first heard she was back, I thought about her mom and when they lived here. I didn't know what to expect. But she's turned out pretty great. She's…"

"She's special."

Dad looks at me and smiles. "Yeah, I suppose she is."

We work on the car. We go to Lowes and we get lunch and it's probably one of the best days my dad and I have enjoyed together in a while. He doesn't get on me about a job, doesn't say a word about college or school or anything really. He talks about the car—a lot about the car.

Still determined not to sulk about Lia, I throw myself into getting the grass cut and then go for a run. A few miles, one foot then the other, keep chugging along so my brain doesn't catch up with me. It works, I run myself into the ground. Until I get home and crash in the den.

I dream about the treasure. I'm roaming through the woods, tripping over the limbs and tangles of brush, and Lia is nowhere to be found. I'm chasing the clues, trying to understand the notes so I can find her.

Because she is the treasure.

I STARTLE AWAKE when the phone rings.

"Hello?"

A moan on the other end, followed by Lia's warbled voice. "Matthew."

At first I think it's the connection, but then she sniffles and lets out a groan. I jump to my feet. "Lia, what's going on?"

Breathing. Wet, ragged, breathing. Again she starts to say something but it catches.

"Lia, please. What's happening?"

"She did it again." Her voice crumbles.

I wipe my face. More noises I can't understand. The phone scraping her cheek. But I don't have to ask what she did or who *she* is. I stuff my feet in my shoes and go looking for a hoodie. "Lia, where are you? I'll come get you. Are you in Stetson?"

Some fumbling on her end, another groan. "No. My car broke down. I'm in…" A quiver in her breath before she breaks down all over again.

My whole body tingles. "Lia, please. Where are you?"

"We had a really good day. Really good. Then I left that night. We were supposed to go to…" She sucks in a breath. "She stole some money. She just took it and…" Her voice breaks off. "She's back in jail, Matthew. I don't know what I did."

My eyes fill with tears. I run a hand through my hair. "You did everything, Lia. This is not your fault, okay. Please tell me where you are."

In the laundry room, I throw on the hoodie, check the clock. After falling asleep I'm disoriented. But it's only six-thirty in the evening. "Lia?"

"Tennessee? Virginia? I'm at a gas station. My car is shot. They said…"

Searching for my keys, I find Mom and Dad in the kitchen. Seeing the shape I'm in, half dressed and pacing around, they demand to know what's going on. "It's Lia. Her car broke down. I'm going to get her."

Dad looks at Mom. "I'll go with you."

"Dad, no."

Lia falls apart in my ear. Dad tells me he's coming and that's it. Ten minutes later I'm still talking with Lia as we get in the car and head west.

Chapter 38

Dad hits the freeway in a hurry. Lia's too big of a mess to talk much, but I manage to get some basic directions out of her—landmarks, mile markers. She's right outside of Bristol. She says the gas attendant is hanging out in the shop until we make it.

Dad grimaces. "Bristol?"

I nod. "Near I-381, Route Eleven. A Marathon station."

"At least she's not on the side of the road."

"Yeah."

We fly past Roanoke. Dad slugs down convenience store coffee and drives like it's his life's mission. I call Lia back. She's not doing any better.

Once we're on I-81, Dad hits the gas and we're really moving. We pass truck after truck until we find 381 and after getting turned around and restarting and wasting about fifteen minutes, we find Junction I-11. We pass a carwash, a storage place, a few abandoned brick buildings. Then my heart about leaps out of my chest at the sight of the Marathon station.

"Dad, right there. Right there!"

Dad leans forward. "I see her, Matt."

He pulls in, and I leap from the truck. I run to Lia's car as her door opens and she spills into my arms, a heap of hair and choking sobs. "Oh, Matthew. Please help me. It hurts so much."

Tears roll down my cheeks. My body tingles with shock at the sound of her raw emotion. Wet, shaky breaths in the crook of my neck. She's come completely apart, and all I can do is hold her up, draw her into me.

Dad stands a few feet away as the guy from the station hustles out, his shoulders square and looking like he's going to run us off before he realizes we're who she's been waiting for.

He calls out to Dad. "She wouldn't come in. I tried. I didn't want to leave her." He looks back to the garage. "I stayed."

Dad thanks the guy. I scoop Lia up and carry her to the truck, where I set her in the backseat. Then I go back for her bag, her phone, whatever else she might need while Dad and the guy peek under the hood.

I get back to Lia, curled into the backseat. She's shaking violently, her entire body shuddering as I wrap her in the blanket Dad was thoughtful enough to pack. I pull her close, slip my arm around her and hold her.

Eventually Dad gets back into the truck. "Well, uh, bad news, about the car, that is. The engine block is cracked. Probably more than it's worth. He says he can tow it, but..."

Lia looks up, her voice small and strained. "It's okay. We can leave it."

Dad looks at me through the mirror. I nod. He gets out, talks to the guy again, then walks back to the truck.

"He says," Dad stops short, looks down, then nods. "Okay then, let's get you home, Lia."

And we pull away quietly, leaving Lia's broken little car, the guy watching us, Lia seeing nothing, her head buried in my side as the streetlights pass over us in the dark.

THE RIDE BACK IS QUIET. The low hum of the radio the only sound as Dad sits at the wheel mechanically, with the occasional turn of the head to pass slower traffic as I hold onto Lia, who's still trembling. She clings to me the entire way.

It's around two in the morning when we get home. And even Dad realizes we're not dropping Lia off at her house to be alone.

I help her inside, the blanket draped over her shoulders. Mom is up in an instant, but one look at Lia and her face goes tight and her eyes are glossy. I help Lia to the guest room, kiss her forehead, and let her sleep.

Mom waits for me in the kitchen, the low light coming from the lamp in the corner. "Matt, what in the world?"

I shake my head. "Her mom is back in jail. She doesn't want to talk about it."

"Oh my word." Mom sucks in a breath. "That poor, poor girl."

Dad, standing at the counter, the lines on his face outlining his exhaustion, agrees. "She's awfully tore up. It makes you wonder how a parent can do that."

I nod and thank Dad for driving, for understanding. For everything. And then I go off to bed, a wall away from Lia and all that hurt she's carrying.

Chapter 39

By morning Lia is gone. A thank you note sits on the table. I head up the street, grab two coffees, then go down to check on her.

I knock but there's no answer. I peek in and call for her, but the house is silent. Something makes me look back, to the path, and I turn and walk down to the pond.

She sits on the edge of the dock. Her hair is up, out, wildly tangled and beautiful. A stick snaps beneath my foot and she turns. When she sees me she tries her best to smile, but her lips fail to make the trip. I walk up and sit beside her, offer her the coffee.

She closes her eyes and whispers. "Thanks."

"Lia, I'm so, so sorry. Really, it's..."

She sets her head against my shoulder. "I'm not sure I can cry anymore. It's like I've run out of tears."

We gaze out to the mirror of water, the morning sun throwing shafts into the ripples. The ducks aren't around, maybe they're in the forest, hopefully. I don't think Lia can take much more disappointment today. We sit quietly. I figure she'll talk about it when she's ready. I only want to be with her right now, absorb some of the hurt that's weighing her down.

Another sip of coffee and she sits up a little straighter. "So, we did the fishing thing, like I told you. And then I went to the outlet stores and bought her a pair of Gap jeans, a few tops, because she didn't have much to wear."

A leaf makes a lazy plummet to pond's surface. It spins slowly, floating, as Lia wipes her face and stares out at the water. "She was so excited about it, about trying on clothes and spending time with me.

She was talking about getting a waitressing job, and I told her that was great, just great. It was like I was the parent, and that was okay because she was clean and working to get better. She was trying, you know?"

I wipe my eyes, unable to hold it back.

Lia blows on her coffee but keeps her gaze on the water without wiping the tears tracing down her face. I wonder if she even knows she's crying anymore. "At least that's what I thought. So that night, she was wearing her new jeans and we were playing Uno on the bed. I was telling her about the play and how great it went, and..." Lia lets out a hiccup of a gasp. She turns to me. "It just wasn't enough for her, Matthew."

I pull her closer. "It's not your fault, Lia."

She shakes her head as though forcing herself to get through it, pulls away from me and exhales. "So, nine o'clock rolls around. Visiting hours are over, and I had a bad feeling about it, something about how fidgety she was getting. She wasn't listening to me, her eyes were somewhere else, even when I told her I'd see her in the morning. I was pleading, like, we'll go shopping again, I'll blow every bit of money I have if..."

She sets her quivering chin to her chest. I gaze across the pond, to the giant sycamore tree on the rock, it's branches spreading over the pond, over us.

Lia, still determined to get through it, raises her head. "And then I noticed some money was missing." Her face balls up. "Everything I had left. Twenty-five hundred for bail, two thousand down for treatment. She took the last few hundred bucks I had, besides a few twenties I'd tucked away for gas. I was about to go back, find a way to confront her about it, but they're tight about visits and I told myself maybe, maybe I left it. I tossed and turned over it, until I the call came at five in the morning. She was gone, checked herself out and left in a cab."

She turns to me, brow furrowed, nose bunched up as though

struggling to understand. Her voice only a whisper now. "She stole money from me when I would've given it to her. She didn't even ask me. She stole the..."

She falls into me, banging her fists on my chest. "I looked everywhere, walking into restaurants. I hoped..." She pulls back, looking at me, the tears spilling from her eyes. "I thought maybe she was applying for jobs." She shakes her head.

Between crying jags, Lia explains how by two o'clock that afternoon, her mom was in jail for violating probation.

She sniffles. "I didn't go. I'm not going. I will never go see her again."

We sip coffee, catch our breaths. After a while, Lia gets up and announces she's done crying for the day. Her face is puffy and red, her hair still a mess. She turns and begs me to distract her.

I am happy to oblige.

We hunt for treasure. I find the shovel and she runs in for her notes and we gather at the old picnic table she makes me drag out into the sun in the middle of the yard. The day is clear and perfect, maybe around sixty degrees. Lia throws herself into this silly treasure hunt, talks about pirates, clouds, stars, and constellations. Lia needs to be Lia right now. She needs to smile in the sun.

This time, as we get closer to the pond, she's all about rocks. "I really think he wanted us to find it, maybe it's a pile of rocks or something obvious."

"Wait, *us*?"

She walks over to me and kisses me. When she pulls away she smiles. "Yes, *us*. You've said it before. He was trying to reunite us."

"Well, it worked."

"It did, didn't it?"

I nod, looking into her eyes.

She smiles the real smile, and it's something to see. Until she nudges me with her shoulder. "Now, come on, this way."

So we look for piles of rocks, or what Lia thinks looks like piles of rocks. I try to imagine Preacher Higgins roaming these woods, a sack on his back, a shovel in his hand, searching for the perfect spot to hide his treasure.

The tree and the rock. The tree and the rock. Mirrors. Madness. Whatever she wants.

Again, nothing. We break that afternoon, still no closer to finding anything. Lia shrugs and says she's tired of digging. I don't remind her I'm doing the digging.

We get to the door and she turns to me. "I need to go thank your parents for everything."

"Yeah, okay. My mom will want to feed you though. You want to eat dinner with us?"

She nods. "Yeah, let me go shower and change. Do you want," she looks at the house, bites her lip in a way that's irresistible. "Do you want to wait, or...?"

"Yeah." I nod. "I mean, I don't... Yeah."

She laughs. We get inside and I sit on the couch. Fremont jumps on my lap.

Lia says, "Home sweet home," and starts down the hall. Then she turns around and walks back into the room. She leans down and kisses me on the lips. "Thanks for everything, Matthew."

I nod without words. Lia laughs again, a finger tracing my lips as she slowly pulls away. I'm in a trance of sorts so I don't notice her expression until she makes a small sound. She cocks her head one way then the other, studying the painting on the mantel. I'm smiling like a fool and Fremont is purring and I'm only happy she's at least trying to put herself together, when she gasps.

"What?"

Her mouth falls open. She looks at me, and I can't tell if she's messing with me or not when she walks to the mantel and stops again. She stands straighter then leans forward. Closer still, inches from it, before she takes a step back and makes another sound.

Fremont hops down. I get to my feet. "Lia, what is it?"

She reaches out as I sidle up behind her and follow her index finger to the painting. Past the boy and the girl to the shaft of sun on the water, where it leads to...

Lia whispers. "The tree..."

"The rock."

"The sun, the reflection, it's..."

"It's right there."

She turns to me, then back to the painting where now I can't unsee it. It's like an arrow, pointing directly to the sycamore tree, or the rock beneath the sycamore tree.

She leaps in place, Fremont yowls. "The painting is the map!"

I look at her, then back to the painting. It's all right there. I'm still staring when she takes my wrist and drags me out the door. "Come on, get the shovel. We've found it!"

I chase after her, tripping over a planter as I snatch up the shovel. My mind buzzes, and part of me says this can't be real as my feet move to keep up with Lia, who's faster than most of the linebackers I've gone against.

At the dock, she flies to a halt and I nearly crash into her. Her head goes right to left, then... "There."

I follow her finger across the pond, to the huge tree. And there it is, the tree and the rock. It has to be the place, I mean, if there is "a place," this is it. I turn to her and she squeals then starts around the pond, and I'm reminded of when Lia took me back here three years ago, before we knew the preacher. It was midnight and she basically dragged me around to where he was sleepwalking.

Now, as she tears through the thickets and briars all over again, I'm wondering if what we saw in the painting is as real as it looked. Either way, it's exactly what she needs right now. Treasure or not, it's a beautiful distraction.

She scampers up the hill to the tree, causing an avalanche of dirt and leaves and small pebbles. Throwing back her hair, she looks at me as I struggle with the roots and the loose footing she's left behind.

I'm sort of worried about snakes, but I don't say it to her. Beneath the giant roots of the tree is a rock, hanging over the dirt.

Lia points. "This is it, Matthew." She leans over and kisses me forcefully. I'm momentarily lost, until she gives my arm a shake. "Okay, now dig! Here, no, here!"

She starts clawing away at the dirt. I remind her I brought a shovel. She stops, wipes her hands on her khaki shorts, and nods like a lunatic. "Yeah, yeah, yeah."

A thrust into the dirt, the earth is dark and the digging is easy. I scoop out a few shovelfuls and toss them to the side. It scatters down the hill, and I plunge the shovel in deeper, a couple of feet down, and again, scooping, an avalanche of dirt flowing down the bank, plip-plopping into the pond. Then I hit something. Not a rock, but something softer.

"Stop!"

I laugh. "I've already stopped."

She doesn't hear me as she throws herself in, scraping out handfuls of dirt. She's got dirt under her nails and bits on her arms. The birds chirp, the critters buzz, as Lia digs and I bend down and join in and we both feel it, and she starts tugging and it's round, cylindrical, blue, and...

A big coffee tin. Maxwell house, like the ones that line the basement. A few spots of rust. "I don't believe it. Lia, it's really here."

She smiles big, talking fast. "I know, I know. I knew it was." She pulls it out and wipes it off, looks at me with wide eyes. "It's heavy."

I fall beside her in the dirt, holding my breath as she peels off the plastic lid. Our heads come together as we lean closer. It's wrapped in cloth. Lia reaches in. "Feels like money."

"Pull it out."

With a smile, she pulls out the cloth and sets it on her lap. "This is crazy."

She takes one end and peels it back, and we find ourselves looking at several stacks of curled bills. Lia looks up at me.

I look around, then back to the can. "Is it, is that real?"

Her face is a beautiful smudgy mess. "How should I know?"

She holds up a stack of bills bound by a rubber band. Hundreds, fifties, twenties. I swallow down whatever else I was going to say, which is nothing, because the treasure was real all along.

Chapter 40

Eighty-three-thousand dollars. Cash. It sits on the table along with the dented coffee can, the clues, the notes, and the painting leaning up against the wall. Lia's uncharacteristically quiet. But what is there to say?

I flop over a stack of bills. "Um, so, either Higgins was really good at betting on horses, or he was in the mafia."

She stares at the money, blankly, her body drained, having been a conduit of every human emotion available in the span of twenty-four hours.

I scratch my head. "Lia?"

I sit down, take her hand, use my other hand to gesture over the treasure. "So while most people make a will, which he did, Mr. Higgins also buried a treasure, painted a map, and left clues for you to find it."

She turns to me. "Does he know me, or what?"

And once again I want to say something like my dad would say, about how this is her future or something corny. Especially when her smile vanishes and her eyes lose their flash. It hits me like a punch.

I squeeze her hand. "Hey, I know what you're thinking. Bail. Rehab. Help for your mom, right?"

Her eyes well.

I hate myself for bringing it up. "Lia, please don't do this to yourself. One, your mom probably can't make bail right now, no matter how much money you have. Besides, you've done everything you can, okay?" She looks at me and I give her hand another squeeze. "Higgins wanted you to have this. He wanted *you* to have this."

She shakes her head slowly. "I don't know what to do now," she says with a sad laugh. Again, she eyes the money. "I mostly just liked the treasure hunting."

Now I'm laughing. "Lia, you found eighty-thousand dollars."

She squeezes my hand. "*We*. We found it. It's half yours."

"My cut was two percent, remember? And I'm, what's the word? I'm *bequeathing* it to you. This is all yours. Not your mom's. Not mine. This is your money. Besides, I'll go treasure hunting with you anytime."

She laughs, falls into me, then extracts herself. "What in the world?"

"You need to call that Sterling dude, okay?"

"And your dad. I want to buy my car back."

That's a good idea, calling my parents. We need to talk to someone, because neither of us have any idea what to do with cash found in a coffee can on the property given to you by a dead preacher. But for a bit longer, we're content to wait. To sit and stare at the money, at the painting. To bask in the awe of Higgins' genius.

But I can tell it's getting to her. How could it not? Her mother took her best intentions, balled them up, and threw them away. Eighty-thousand dollars can't fix that, not for someone like Lia.

So for an hour we hold off on bringing anyone else into this. I listen as she talks about lockdown facilities that could help her mom. And I don't say a word against it, not now, because it's a no-win outcome for her. If she helps her mom, she'll get hurt again and again. If she doesn't, she'll hurt from guilt and regret.

Eventually she calls Sterling and leaves a message. Ten minutes later, we're sitting on the floor of the living room when he calls back. Lia takes the call on speaker and explains about the cash. Well, tries to explain, but it's Lia so she takes the long way and describes every single detail about our treasure hunting adventure.

Sterling listens patiently. When she gets to the part about the money, he sighs. "Well, thank goodness."

Lia and I glance at each other. Lia looks to the phone. "What?"

"You found it. I was beginning to worry."

Again, Lia looks at me and mouths, "What?"

Sterling laughs. "Higgins knew you would, but I must admit, I wasn't so sure. It's a rather unorthodox way to leave someone money, to say the least."

Lia laughs. "I'm um, I'm confused."

"Well, I'll be down shortly to explain the finer points, Miss Lia, but what you need to know right now is that this has all been taken care of. I don't recommend you spend a dime, it's technically in a trust. Had you not found it, I would have dug it up myself on your eighteenth birthday."

Lia's eyes double in size. She looks at me as Sterling rambles on. "This was, no doubt, the oddest bit of probate I've ever done, and I've done some rather wild things in my line of work. Anyways, I can place it in one of several different options I'll lay out for you when I visit. Ways to make the most out of..."

He starts in about interest rates and deductions for a good five minutes, while Lia and I stare at the painting, lost in the craziness of such an elaborate plan.

The next call is to Mom and Dad. We meet them out front, although it's obvious we've already blown to bits the don't-go-inside rule.

My parents approach Lia carefully, remembering the hurt from last night. Lia and I are a bit too excited, all stirred up about finding a treasure—even if it was one she would have gotten eventually anyway.

"Okay, so remember the treasure hunt?" I ask Mom.

She nods and Lia takes my hand. Dad's face goes tight—maybe we're not so sneaky.

Lia blurts out. "Well, guess what?"

Mom and Dad look at each other. Lia squeals, then throws open the door. Dad looks at me.

"You're going to have to see this to believe it," I say.

We lead them to the kitchen table where the old preacher wrote sermons, notes, and most likely, clues to a treasure.

Dad stops. "Holy sh—"

Mom coughs.

Dad looks at Lia, to me, then back to the table. "Is this...is this real?"

Lia picks up a wad of hundred dollar bills and fans it like a game show hostess. "According to my lawyer, it is. Can you believe this?"

"I thought you guys were pulling my leg. I thought it was code or something." Mom shakes her head.

I feel myself blushing at the thought of Mom thinking maybe treasure hunting was code for making out. Although, not a bad idea.

Dad steps forward. "This is incredible." He reaches for a stack. "Can I?"

Lia shrugs. "Be my guest."

We marvel over the cash for a while, then Dad, well, becomes Dad. "So you know this is going to have several tax implications, the IRS and..."

"Dad, seriously. Lia's got a fancy, big-time lawyer handling things."

Lia slaps my arm. Mom looks around the kitchen. And that's when Lia's guilt comes back to haunt her. I can see it in her eyes.

Dad never takes his eyes off the money. "Lia, this is, this is life changing."

Mom steps forward, and once again, for all their faults, I realize how fortunate I am to have such people in my life.

Lia looks to the floor. "I can't stop thinking about my mom. Even after everything. She's sick, you know?"

Mom steps forward. "Lia, please. Please, sweetheart. Please take this gift and don't look back. I've seen you onstage, it's where you belong. This"—she nods to the money—"is a means to get you where you need to be."

Lia stares at the bills, tears threatening her eyes. And I know Higgins did the right thing, leaving her this, even if it's tearing her apart at the moment. Finally, she turns to us. "I just, how can I turn my back on her like that? How can I take this and *not* help?"

As Lia breaks down all over again, Mom takes her in her arms. "This is your turn, Lia. You've given all you can give." She holds Lia tight as she looks up and nods for Dad and me to give them some space.

We step outside, where a slight breeze knocks around some leaves in the yard.

"Wow." Dad raises his eyebrows.

"Yeah."

"This is something else. I wouldn't believe it if I weren't seeing it."

"I know."

There's something unsaid between us. Dad feels it too, when he turns to me. "What a wild twenty-four hours, huh?"

The mosquitoes are out, feasting on my arms.

Dad looks out to the car he and Mom drove down. "So, it was in the painting, huh? That old man sure had some tricks up his sleeve, I'll give him that."

I nod. "I feel bad. I never really thought there was a treasure, you know?"

Dad laughs, then gets serious again. "She'll have to keep this quiet. A place like Maycomb, you know, if people catch wind of this they'll show up in droves. It'll be like the Beale treasure."

I remember hearing stories about the Beale treasure, supposedly buried somewhere in Bedford. I hadn't thought about that, or about word spreading around town. Maybe the news. Then I think about Lia's mom finding out about the money, and I hate myself for imagining such bad things about someone Lia cares about so much.

Dad reads my thoughts. "She's got a lot to think about."

I nod.

"But hey, not a bad haul. I'd say you two are a couple of pirates."

"Please don't do the pirate voice, Dad."

"No?"

I shake my head. "No."

Chapter 41

So how do you show up to school after finding eighty grand in the dirt?

Cold. Lia still refuses to put the top up, choosing instead to blast the heat to fight off the morning chill. We pull into a spot, she puts the car in park and sits back and looks me over with a smile. "And you didn't believe me about the treasure."

I shake my head. This is only the thousandth time she's rubbed it in since Sunday. Sterling arrived yesterday—the guy with all the answers. Lia skipped school, and they got the car titled (all Dad would tell me is that they worked something out), squared away other loose ends, and he even took some time to answer some legal questions about her mother.

The money is sitting in a bank account. From there it will go into a trust fund she can't touch until she's eighteen. Her mom is facing serious time after her last violation. Like we figured, bail was denied. It broke Lia to hear it, I know she's full of regrets and guilt, but for now, it's time Lia thinks about what's best for Lia.

I shrug. "I never said I didn't believe. I was just more prepared than you for it not to exist."

"Ha!" She smiles big, the morning sun playing tricks with her eyes. I can't wait for her to go talk to Mrs. Morgan, to get back into the auditorium where she belongs. She takes my hand, and even though I was at her house until ten last night, it sends a wave of electricity through my limbs. "You, Matthew Crosby, are something special."

Not even close. But if Lia Banks wants to believe I'm special, who am I to disagree? I stare off past the glimmer of sun bouncing off the cars in the parking lot. I look back at Lia and give her a big smile. "I suppose I am, huh?"

Lia shakes her head. "Okay, Mr. I-Was-in-the-Paper. Let's get you out of the car while your head can still fit into the school."

"You saw that?"

"Mr. Wood gave me a copy."

We step out of the car. Austin and the guys nod to us. Jen and Sarah wave. Lia sets her hand in mine, and we start for Maycomb High. Lia, at Maycomb High School. I pull her toward me and our shoulders touch. If nothing else than to be sure it's true.

She looks up at me. "Careful, Crosby, there's a no hugging rule in place."

I look her over. "Did you just call me Crosby?"

She bites her smile. "Hey, I'm trying to fit in around here."

I laugh. Pull her in again. "Good luck with that."

We found the treasure. Lia has a college fund. I could get a scholarship. Both of us now with big plans to wow the world. But for now, starting today, Lia will meet with Mrs. Jackson during her gym period, to talk about *things*, as she tells me.

I hope it's to talk about how to cope with her mother, with addiction. And while it seems like she has it all now—money, house, car, a future on the stage—she would trade it away in a second to have her mom to herself. The pain in her sobs the other night, how it shook through her entire body, it's not a wound that will heal anytime soon.

So Lia and I walk into school together, like some kind of dream. After that I'll go to football practice and be a caveman while she'll go to the auditorium with Mrs. Morgan. To do what she was born to do.

And then?

And then we'll feed her goat, tend to her ducks. Maybe she'll get those chickens. And maybe eventually, hopefully, she will begin to feel better about herself and her future. Maybe we'll go searching for more treasure—her eyes lit up when I told her about the Beale treasure—or maybe we'll do something completely ordinary.

Only it won't be, because I'll be with her, and when you're with Lia, nothing is ever ordinary.

Acknowledgments

Upon reading an early version of this book, my stepmother and mentor, Diane Fanning, said something to the effect of being a sap for romance. My initial reaction was disbelief. I'm sorry, what? I don't write romance.

But she was right. It's a love story. I guess it always had been. So thanks, Diane. I guess it wasn't the first time you've held me accountable for my actions.

Thanks to Nicola Molyneux, across the pond, for always being so eager to read and critique. Thanks to all the reviewers who appreciated Treehouse and its slow journey. It was your kind words that pushed me to continue Matt and Lia's journey.

Thanks to Staci Olsen and Holli Anderson for everything. For being in my corner, for fixing my errors, and for standing behind all eleven books we've done together. You guys are the best.

Thanks to Simon, the coolest kid I know. To Bella, my wild and crazy character who's never met a sunrise she couldn't liven up with a little running and shouting. Lastly, thanks to Anne, for believing in me and my writing.

About the Author

Pete Fanning is the author of *Justice in a Bottle* and *Runaway Blues*. He lives in Virginia with his wife, son, baby girl, and two very spoiled dogs. He can be found at www.petefanning.com, where he's posted over 200 flash fiction stories.

This has been an
Immortal Production

CPSIA information can be obtained
at www.ICGtesting.com
Printed in the USA
BVHW062331060123
655722BV00003B/566

9 781953 491473